The Dragon Children

by Bryan Buchan
illustrated by Kathryn Cole

Scholastic Book Services

New York · Toronto · London · Auckland · Sydney · Tokyo

Copyright © 1972 by Bryan Buchan. All rights reserved.

Canadian Cataloguing in Publication Data

Buchan, Bryan, 1945-
   The dragon children

ISBN 0-590-71089-3

I. Title.

PS8553.U33D72   jC813'.54   C76-2633-5
PZ7.B83Dr
4th printing 1986   **Printed in Canada**

contents

FOR SCOTT AND ANDREW

To catch a crook

That rain sure felt icy cold against my neck. I hunched up my shoulders and muttered at myself for being so stupid. The day before I'd been swimming in the shallows of the river and had gone home without my towel. It was just a worn-out old rag, really, with a big hole and a paint stain, but today Mother had sent me back to find it.

It was a lot cooler than yesterday and rain had been falling ever since I'd pulled myself out of bed.

The towel was still draped over the cedar branch where I'd left it. Stopping only to wring the water out, I headed gloomily back along the river trail, mud squishing into my running shoes at each step. Wet branches rubbed across my face, and the smell of damp woodland soil and cedar surrounded me. That smell always made me feel lonely, but also kind of happy, and I began to think the trip hadn't been so terrible after all. Before long I started to enjoy the feel of the misty drizzle and the sound of little drops of water falling from twig to twig in the damp cedar trees.

At school I was always in the middle of things and liked it. But suddenly it was fun to feel all alone in the greyness of the rain.

I wasn't far from civilization, of course. The narrow strip of trees we call the woods runs for maybe half a mile along the north shore of the river. It's only a narrow strip, filling the space between River Road, where my house is, and the river itself. If you walked through the cedar woods from the river, you would reach my street and then the rest of our town, north of my house. South of the river is another group of houses along Bridge Road, and then nothing but open fields until you get to the bypass.

I can't really be sure when I first realized I was not alone. Several times I thought someone was creeping silently along beside me through the trees, but when I halted for a closer look the bush around me was deserted, or so it seemed. I hurried a little, afraid that someone was shadowing me. My best friend, Graham, had once been beaten up right around here by a tough gang of older boys, and I didn't want to run into them. I wasn't afraid of any of the bullies at school, and I'd been in plenty of fights, but I knew I couldn't handle five kids all several years older than me. And the boys who had ambushed Graham hadn't been fair fighters, believe me.

Whoever it was, managed to move silently among the trees, and no matter how hard I tried I couldn't see him — or them. A few times, out of the corner of my eye, I thought I saw someone sneaking along between the trail and the river. But whenever I turned my head there was no one there — only a funny feeling that a moment before someone *had* been there.

Finally I lost control and bolted. Home was less than a couple hundred yards away; I was almost within yelling distance. Faster and faster I raced along the trail, the dripping branches slapping my face until my eyes watered and I could scarcely see.

A twisted cedar root stretched across the trail roughly grabbed my ankle. I sprawled full length into the dirt on the path. For a second or two I lay absolutely still, my face in the soft black mud, waiting for the attack I was sure would follow. *Catch the enemy off guard,* I repeated to myself. Maybe I could surprise those bullies by playing dead.

Nothing happened.

At last, cautiously, I lifted my head, hardly daring to breathe. I was entirely alone.

I groaned, not in pain, but in utter disgust. I wasn't hurt, but my clothes were a rich chocolate colour, like the cedar-strewn muck in the path. There was a mushy sucking sound as I pushed my chest up out of the mud.

Then I saw him. Right in front of me, about five feet away, were two scruffy brown shoes. My eyes moved gradually upward until I took in his whole length.

The boy was tall, fair and on the thin side. His hair was the colour of new plywood, and his face was dotted with a million freckles. He was smiling strangely, and his grey eyes looked as though he was about to laugh. He didn't look the least bit like a bully.

But the oddest thing was his clothing. He had faded blue jeans, with heavy patches on the knees. All the boys I knew wore blue jeans, but his were different. They were rolled up at the bottom to make cuffs that reached halfway to his knees; the insides of the jeans were lined with fuzzy plaid material. He had no belt. Elastic and leather suspenders, like those the clowns wear in the circus, held the pants up. Tucked into them was a heavy flannel shirt in very nearly the same plaid as the cuffs. None of the boys at my school would ever dress like that. He must be a visitor from a different town, I decided, maybe from another province.

The strange boy squatted down cheerfully in front of me, and his grin became even wider. I wasn't afraid of him at all.

"Hello, John," he said.

"Hey!" I squawked. "How do you know my name?"

He laughed. "The wind told me. Are you going to get up out of that puddle?"

I scrambled quickly to my feet and started to wipe the muck off my face and chest with the towel.

"How do you know who I am?" I asked again. He

only grinned. It was plain he didn't intend to tell me. I decided to change the question.

"What's *your* name?" I demanded. "And where do you live?"

"My name is Steven," the boy replied. "I used to live near here, south of town, on the south bank of the river." His face lost its grin, and his eyes became cloudy looking. "But I left a very long time ago. Sometimes I can come back to visit."

Steven's voice trailed off wistfully and for a few seconds he was silent. Then he brightened up and the grin returned. He spoke excitedly, as though he had been waiting a long time to tell someone his secret. "Today, though, I have something really important to do. That's why I hurried back. That's why I was following you along the trail. I have to find someone trustworthy to help me catch a crook."

"Have you considered the police?" I asked, trying to hide a hint of sarcasm.

"No," Steven answered. That was all: no explanation, no excuses, no reason why the police shouldn't get mixed up with the case. He had such a funny expression on his face that I didn't press him. I felt just the way I had when he didn't answer my first question, about my name. He was obviously a mysterious kid, and I liked mysteries well enough to avoid ruining this one.

"I don't think I'd be any good at catching crooks," I suggested modestly, and immediately regretted my

11

words. I was afraid he might agree and leave me wondering about the whole thing. "Although I did go with my class to tour the police station last fall," I added quickly.

Already I was growing more than a little curious — I've always had trouble walking away from puzzles. What did this kid with the funny clothes know about crooks? And more important, how did he know my name?

Steven only smiled patiently. I knew I was eager to help him, and I guess he did too.

"First of all," he said, "we have to gather as much evidence as we can. I've already found out a lot about what the thief has been doing on this side of the river. You'll have to investigate the houses across the bridge, along Bridge Road."

"Why did you only do this side? Didn't you say you used to live south of the river?" I knew somehow that this too was a stupid question.

"I can't cross the river now." Again Steven looked unhappy.

"You can't cross the river?" I asked, not sure that I understood him correctly. "Why not?"

"I used to cross it all the time, when I came in to the village to go to school. Only I can't now, that's all." I thought maybe he was going to cry, he had such a funny look on his face.

Crumbs! what a weird kid, I thought to myself. I

supposed his mother wouldn't let him cross the bridge, although he was about the same age as me. But it was clear that I wasn't likely to get any more information by questioning him.

"Anyway, John, we'll work together on this case. I can't catch him without your help, so you're stuck, pal." Somehow, when Steven said it, that ridiculous statement made sense. If I had realized then the terrible problems, the embarrassment and danger it would lead to, I would have run like crazy for home.

"The crook is a real swindler, John, a confidence man. He finds old people, people who live alone, and tells them all kinds of terrible things. When he gets them really frightened, he takes their money and disappears."

"Why don't they report him to the police if he takes their money?" That question, at least, sounded reasonable.

"Sometimes they don't know they've been cheated. He swindles them so well they never realize he's a phony. Some of them can't even leave the house, and no one ever comes to visit them, except the occasional deliveryman. Maybe they're too proud to ask for help and just try to keep everything quiet. And sometimes I think they're just too embarrassed to admit they were fooled. It's up to us to help them."

Normally I would have wondered why it was up to us, but I only asked, "And how are we going to do that, Steven?"

13

Before he could answer, I heard the voice of my seven-year-old brother, Scott, calling me from farther down the trail.

"That's my little brother," I confessed. "He probably wants me to come home for lunch."

I turned around and caught sight of Scott running down the trail towards us. Even when he saw me, he still shrieked, "Jo-ohn! Jo-ohn!"

It was obvious from the racket he was making that the rain had resulted in a whole morning of "quiet games" under Mother's supervision, and that he needed to release some of his usual energy.

Scott wasn't a bad little kid, really. He was good at keeping secrets, and he never snitched on me unless he had to. We didn't look like brothers, though, because he was so dark. His hair and eyes were almost black, and his skin looked as though he had just returned from the West Indies. He was tall for his age and was usually grinning, although right then he was annoyed about getting wet in the drizzle.

"Hey, John!" he bellowed at me from about four feet away. "What are you doing out here in the rain so long?"

"I'm speaking with a friend," I answered, trying to sound grown-up.

"Where is he, then?"

"Right here, stupid," I said, turning back to face Steven. Then I stopped short. There was no one there.

Only a strange scent of pine filled the air.

I stumbled for an explanation. "Well, he was here a minute ago, Scott. He must have gone when he heard you coming. You made enough noise to stampede a herd of elephants. What do you want, anyway?"

Cathy can help

"Mother sent me to find you," Scott insisted. "She was afraid you'd fallen in the river, you were gone so long." His dark eyes were angry and his lower lip stuck out. "Lunch is almost ready. And you have to come quickly, 'cause Cathy is here to stay with us for a while."

"Oh no!" I moaned.

Cathy was my cousin, and ordinarily I wouldn't have minded her visit at all. She was the same age as me and always willing to play ball or climb onto the roof. When she came we usually had a lot of fun. But this time was different. I had a mystery to solve, and Cathy would only be in the way.

"How long is she planning to stay, Scott?" I asked, hoping she was slated to leave right after lunch.

"I don't know. Hurry up, won't you," he groaned. "I'm getting all wet. Just 'cause you fell in the mud doesn't mean I have to get soaked, you know."

Scott was right. The rain had let up, but it was still

16

drizzling. I realized I was drenched right through to my underwear and was shivering in the cool air. I wondered why I hadn't felt it before.

As we squelched homeward along the trail, I thought of a scheme to keep Cathy busy while I investigated the crook. I laid my arm across Scott's shoulder, forgetting for the moment that I was covered in mud. He pushed me away indignantly. "Get your soppy old hand off me."

This was not quite the reaction I had been hoping for. Scott would usually do whatever you told him to, but he could be unpredictable. Sometimes he'd follow you around like a puppy dog, without questioning anything. At other times he'd get stubborn and demanding. I had to revise my plans, it seemed, since he was in one of those moods.

"Just being friendly, Scott, old pal."

I tried to look and sound as though my feelings were hurt, but he didn't seem too sympathetic. He bounced along the trail ahead of me, keeping himself out of reach.

"I thought about lending you my new bike," I continued. "I was even going to lower the seat just so you could ride it."

Interest glinted in Scott's eyes as he turned back to me. "Your new bike? Really?" His voice sounded every bit as eager as I had hoped. Maybe I would be able to get Cathy out of the way after all.

"And I know how you could have a good time with the bike, Scott," I purred.

"How?" The suspicion was completely gone from his voice, and he was his usual eager self. I felt guilty for taking him in so easily.

"You could ride out to the conservation area," I suggested brightly. It was Scott's favourite picnic area, because there was a huge hollow tree you could climb from inside. "The rain's stopping, so you could even go this afternoon." He was all ears. "With Cathy."

Scott's jaw fell. "What?" he squeaked. "Aren't you coming?"

"Well, Scott, if I went I'd have to ride Cathy double on my bike. You would have to use your own bike instead of my new five-speed racer."

"But my bike has a loose seat," he protested. "The last time I went over a bump it came off and I landed on the crossbar."

"Yes, that would hurt. But since you'd rather have me along to look after you, I'll be needing my bike — with the hand brakes and the battery-powered horn." Scott loved that horn because he could yell and make noise with it all at the same time. He looked crestfallen, and for a moment I felt guilty about using him that way. He was, after all, just a little kid.

"Mother would probably give you and Cathy a whole bunch of peanut butter cookies to take," I added. "It would be a lot of fun, especially with the new bike."

18

"Do you really think so?" Scott brightened. "Maybe we *will* go by ourselves. But remember, you promised me your bike to use." He bounced around in front of me, even more eager to get home.

"Agreed," I said, as we walked across the last stretch of open field to the house. It was a relief to know that Scott and Cathy would both be out of the way, and that I could safely meet Steven again and continue the investigation. I still didn't know what was expected of me, but now at least I would be able to find out. Scott ran up the steps and through the side door ahead of me.

Mother was getting the soup bowls out. She had stacked a great pile of sandwiches on the table, and everything looked ready — although I didn't see Cathy anywhere.

She wasn't missing for long! As I stepped into the room, she leaped onto my back from her hiding place behind the door. The wrestling match ended quickly enough, though, when she discovered I was coated in muck.

"Yecch!" she said. "What are you doing covered in mud? Can't I even plan a friendly attack without getting all gooey?"

"What are you up to?" I asked.

"Just practising a surprise attack I saw on TV the other night. You let the enemy get past you and then you leap from the rear. Works great," she added, "unless the enemy has been lying in a swamp."

I had seen the same program. Besides, I had once tried a similar tactic on a kid who had been bullying Graham, so I figured I was more expert than Cathy. "Poor technique," I said and made a face at her.

Mother got into the act and sent us all to get cleaned up before lunch. I was ordered to have a bath.

"Don't take too long," she shouted down the hall. "We're ready to eat."

Cathy also had her say. "No time to play with your rubber duckie, John," she yelled.

When I returned, four steaming bowls of soup were lined up in front of the sandwiches.

Scott was peering hopefully at the patches of blue sky outside the window. "Do you want to ride the bikes out to the conservation area?" he asked Cathy. "It's a real neat place."

For a few seconds Cathy thought it over, while trying to float the spoon in her soup. "All right, Scott," she agreed, "but I'm going to have to use your bike, because that old wreck of John's is too hard for me to steer." I half expected Scott to tell her that I had a new bike, but he was alert enough not to spoil his chances.

"You and Scott can ride double on your bike, John," she went on.

"It's not safe to ride double, Cathy," I explained quickly. "But it's all right. That bike of mine will do nicely for Scott, and you can have his. Okay, Scott?" He nodded happily. "I'll just stay home this afternoon,"

I added, coughing weakly and trying to look diseased. "I think I'm getting a cold anyway." Cathy was clearly suspicious and examined my face for clues, but I managed to appear innocent.

Scott had already finished his soup and two sandwiches, and we hurried to catch up with him. He got a fierce look from Mother for blowing bubbles in his milk, so he stopped pretty quickly. Then, with a great snort of satisfaction, he finished his pudding and pushed back his chair. He had chocolate all over his chin and the end of his nose, and wiped it onto the sleeve of his shirt.

He started to say "Hey, Mo—" but burped and halted in embarrassment.

"I beg your pardon," Mother prompted him. In all the years she had been saying that to Scott, I can't recall once that he realized "I beg your pardon" was what *he* was supposed to say. He thought Mother had trouble hearing.

"Hey," he continued eagerly, "can me and Cathy have some peanut butter cookies to take this afternoon? Huh? Huh?"

"No, Scott, I'm sorry," Mother replied. "John ate the last of them this morning, after breakfast." Scott tried to kick my leg under the table. How was I supposed to know those were the last of the cookies?

To avoid having them hanging around any longer, I made a generous offer. "You can have my share of last night's cake, Scott." There was a large chunk of angel food cake which had been saved for me from supper the night before. I was hoarding it as a special treat, but the sacrifice was worth it. The sooner those two left, the faster I could get back to Steven.

Scott was pleased and raced around the kitchen, anxious to get started. "Hurry up, Cathy," he urged.

Before long, Cathy, Scott and my new five-speed racer were headed for Greenwood Conservation Area. Mother made me help her clear the table. There were only a few dishes, so I volunteered to help dry them as well. I didn't want to seem too anxious to get away, in case she got suspicious.

That proved to be a mistake. "Here, John, would you cut off the ends of the rhubarb stalks," Mother said, "and slice them up for the pies." She brought me the bundle and gave me a paring knife. "Be careful you don't cut yourself," she warned, as she sprinkled the counter top with flour and then pressed the rolling pin into a mound of dough.

I had once tried to roll out pastry that way, but it stuck to the roller. When I tried to shake it loose, it flopped into Scott's hair. That was the last time I was given any challenging jobs in the kitchen.

"It's too bad you aren't feeling well, John," Mother said quietly as she rolled out the pie crust. "Where did you put your dirty clothes, by the way?"

"They're in the laundry. And I'm not really sick, I just didn't want to spoil the fun for Scott and Cathy.

We really couldn't ride double, you know, and my old bike is pretty useless."

Mother looked at me suspiciously. She knew how often I had ridden Graham double, and she sighed. "I suppose I should believe you."

"How long is Cathy staying with us?" I asked.

"For the rest of the summer. Uncle Mark is taking a special course in England, and your aunt is going with him. A lady was coming to stay with Cathy, but she fell last night and broke her hip, so I told Aunt Ellen Cathy could stay with us."

The rest of the summer! With the most interesting mystery ever on my hands, I would have Cathy hanging around!

"I think I'll go for a walk," I said, pulling on my boots and a clean jacket. "I'll be back soon."

Darn it all anyhow, I thought to myself as I trudged across the field. How could I keep Cathy out of the way until Steven and I caught the crook? I couldn't palm her off on Scott forever. He was pretty stupid at times, but even a seven-year-old would soon realize what was going on. Maybe she would make friends with some of the girls in town. I would have introduced her before, except I didn't actually get along too well with them.

I wandered along the river trail, still trying to solve this problem. The cedars made the path look gloomy despite the lukewarm sun. In front of me a squirrel leaped from bough to bough along the path, scolding

23

noisily. I glanced down the empty trail, then back to the squirrel. "Hello," I muttered.

"Hello," answered a voice behind me. I wheeled in surprise and there was Steven. His grin was the same as before, and he was still wearing the same funny clothes. His hair and raft of freckles somehow seemed to make the woods a little brighter.

"Don't worry about your cousin," he said. "She'll be really helpful in our investigation."

5K·206

I was amazed. "What do you mean, Cathy's going to help us investigate? How do you know about Cathy?" Steven smiled again, and I knew that no more information on that topic was forthcoming.

"I came to tell you about this crook we're after, John. Then you can start your part of the investigation." He looked very pleased with himself but there was a note of urgency in his voice.

"Okay, Steve, go ahead."

"Well, as I told you, this man is really most interested in retired people, especially those who live by themselves — you know, the ones who have no family around to help them out. He pretends he's a building inspector and checks through the house for things that need repair. He makes a whole bunch of notes in a book and looks very serious. I watched his performance the other day. The guy's a real actor.

"Then he tells the owner that the house is in such bad

repair that he has no choice but to condemn it. He almost looks sorry for what he's doing. He says that the owner will have to move in a few days unless he arranges to have the repairs made."

"What happens then, Steve?"

"The old people are very upset, of course. In some cases they've lived in their houses for fifty years or more and don't want to move. But they can't make the repairs the 'building inspector' says they need, because they're too old or too sick to do the work themselves. And they can't afford to hire carpenters or plumbers or electricians or roofers. They just don't know what to do.

"The crook pretends to be very sympathetic. He hates to see anyone lose his home, he says. So he suggests that for a small fee, much less than a carpenter or a heating specialist would charge, he'll personally see that the house is brought up to standard. He says this is a lot of extra work for him, he has to do it in his spare time, he may even lose on the arrangements, but he's just naturally soft-hearted. He guarantees the house will pass inspection when he's finished.

"Naturally the owner is relieved and agrees to pay more than he can really afford. The crook has pulled this swindle at least four times here. Who knows what he's done on the other side of the river? That's where a lot of older people live, because most of those houses along Bridge Road have been there for ages."

Again Steven looked misty and remote, but I interrupted him with another question. "Does he know how to fix all the things that need fixing? He must be a real handyman, eh?"

Steven looked at me in amazement. "Don't you understand?" he asked irritably. "When this man says he'll repair your chimney or your porch or your attic insulation, say for five hundred dollars, that doesn't mean there is anything wrong with any of it. How many old people will climb up on the roof to see if the shingles really are rotting? How many grandmothers know if their wiring is overloaded?

"So he just bangs around for a while, then tells them the place is repaired and passes inspection, takes the money and disappears. The chimney lasts another eighteen years, which it would have done anyway, and the owner never realizes that it was fine in the first place and that he's been cheated out of a few hundred dollars."

"It doesn't sound very honest to me," I said.

Steven was exasperated. "Of course it isn't honest, John. That's what I've been telling you." He sounded like my mother explaining to Scott why we couldn't go to the beach on a rainy morning.

"Oh. Well then, what should we do now?"

Steven started to sound very professional. "First of all, we finish our investigation. That's where you come in. I imagine the crook keeps his cash with him wherever he's staying. I'll bet he's living at the Star Hotel across the river."

"But don't you remember, Steve?" I asked incredulously. "The Star Hotel burned to the ground when I was a little kid, about five years ago. There was a whole lot of excitement — fire trucks and all kinds of sirens. We could even see the flames from our house. Everyone talked about it for weeks at school."

Steven looked a little confused and wrinkled his nose, making lines across his forehead. "I had forgotten," he explained. "I never get back across there nowadays." A strong smell of pine hung in the air, just as it does in our living room at Christmas time. Steven continued. "Is there any other place where he might be staying?"

"Probably at the new Highway Inn, out near the bypass," I suggested. "It's a big place with a swimming pool and diving boards and tennis courts and everything. Graham and I — that's my buddy who's away on holiday — we went out there when it first opened, and it's a really neat place. Anyhow, it's the only hotel anywhere near here."

Steven was back in charge of the case. "Well then, that's your first assignment, John. Find out if he's staying there. You'll be able to tell by the car. He's been driving a green station wagon, licence number 5K-206. I expect it's a rented car, because he didn't have it when he first showed up. Have you got the licence number?"

I repeated the number several times, just to make

sure. "I'll write it down when I get home. All right, Steve, I'll do my best," I promised. "Should I meet you after supper?"

"Will Scott and Cathy be back from Greenwood in time for you to ride out to the bypass?" asked Steven. I hadn't even remembered that my bicycle was gone.

"Well no," I admitted hesitantly. "I guess not. But I can take my old bike. It's not too far to the Highway Inn, only a couple of miles there and back." It was actually a little farther, I knew, but I didn't want Steven to change his mind.

"Suit yourself, John," he said. "We have to work quickly, though, before he folds up and moves on to another town."

"Right then! See you after supper."

"Good luck, John." Steven grinned and saluted in a funny way. I returned the salute and tried to click my heels together like the soldiers had done on television the other night, but my sloppy old rubber boots just made a weird slurping sound that wasn't very impressive. Then I turned sharply and marched off down the trail toward home.

"Oh, crumbs!" I said out loud. I had forgotten to ask the crook's name. There was now no trace of Steven. Although I called loudly several times, my voice just faded off into the branches along the empty trail. That boy sure could sneak off in a hurry.

When I reached home the smell of rhubarb pie was all

over the place. My mouth was watering, but there wasn't much chance I'd get any pie after guzzling all the cookies. I waited until Mother was busy rearranging the frozen food in the refrigerator, then announced I was going out for a while, but that I'd be back in plenty of time for supper. Mother seldom asked questions when she was busy in the kitchen, and she didn't notice when I slipped out to get my old bike.

I was in the garage before I realized that I had forgotten to write down the licence number Steven had given me. I tore off a bit of blue paper from a fertilizer bag and scribbled the number down with a piece of charcoal.

Leaning against the heap of junk in the back of the garage (the heap that Scott and I were supposed to have cleaned up two weeks ago), I found my old wreck. The front tire was absolutely flat, but I knew it didn't have any fast leaks, so I pumped it up until it was almost normal. Just to be sure, I pumped a few extra times until the tire was a bit larger than the back one. The old crate was functional again. Scott had pirated a handlebar grip to replace one that a boy at school had stolen from his bike, but that really didn't matter. With a little luck it was good enough to get me to the Inn and back.

I pedalled quickly down the driveway and out onto River Street, hoping Mother wouldn't see me and think of something else that had to be done right away. At the end of River Street I turned left and went south on

Bridge Road, across the river and out toward the bypass. The water gurgled cheerfully under the bridge. A wide river that can be rough in the spring when the melt-waters from the hills swell its stream, it's normally very shallow. The bed is rocky and broken by gravel bars, and in several places — which are called "the shallows" — you can walk across on rocks and gravel bars without getting your knees wet. You have to be careful, though, because around many of the shallows are deep potholes, or "wells," where the water is over your head.

On the far side of the bridge the road pokes its way uphill, bordered on each side by tiny frame houses, some of which are as old as the town itself. Many of these houses are run down, but some have beautiful gardens and big lawns.

I always like coming along this part of Bridge Road because the gigantic maple and pine trees tower over my head, making a kind of tunnel. The summertime air is always cool and fresh. In the autumn the leaves turn so bright they make you feel as if you are engulfed by fire; in the spring and early summer the smell of lilac and honeysuckle is overpowering; and in the winter the heavy snow on the tall pines make the road look like a Christmas card.

The hill is steep, and I was pretty well exhausted by the time I reached the top. Without bothering to look where I was, I pulled the bike over to the ditch and lay down in the soft grass under a huge pine tree. The smell of pine resin and the midafternoon warmth made me feel very relaxed. I might have fallen asleep if a pine cone hadn't fallen from one of the very top branches and landed near my head. I wasn't too keen on being bombed, so I sat up to leave. When I saw where I had been resting, I sucked in my breath in surprise.

I wasn't really afraid, just a little taken aback. The pine tree was in front of the place the kids called the Witch's House.

The building itself looked as if it might have come straight out of a horror movie — unpainted boards; ramshackle porch; chimney with missing bricks; rotten shingles; and a shutter that was hanging by its lower hinge only. The garden was a wild tangle of weeds and bushes and the fence was almost hidden by vines and other plants. Everything was in terrible need of tending and repair.

But somehow in the peaceful setting of Bridge Road on a summer afternoon, amidst the pine and grass and the bright shafts of warm sunlight penetrating the leaves, the place wasn't as terrifying as everybody said. No one really believed that the woman who lived there was a witch anyway, but at school there were a lot of strange stories told about her. Some kids said she changed shape or disappeared when she felt like it. Others had seen her hanging around the cemetery all day, just waiting for somebody — or something. They said strange noises emanated from her house at night, lights shone from the rooftop and weird smoke or vapour puffed from the door. Sometimes she could be seen standing in her front yard on a clear night, staring up at the sky.

I wasn't really scared, and I certainly didn't believe those silly stories, but I did feel that it was time to get on with the job I was supposed to be doing. So I pushed off again on my bike, and it creaked and groaned along the crest of the hill as I approached the lip of the south side.

Before starting down I jumped off the bike and stopped for a quick look around. There were no houses on the south slope and few trees. The road ran straight down until it reached the Highway Inn, then turned right to join the bypass. I could see the motel's glass and metal gleaming in the bright sunlight, and the spacious lawns surrounding it. Tiny people were moving about, some playing tennis on the tennis courts. The sun was also reflected from the pool, making it hard to see; but even at that distance I could hear the shouts of people playing in the water.

The Inn was bounded by a tall hedge running along Bridge Road, and the parking lot was partially hidden from view by this hedge. It was difficult for me to tell if there was a green station wagon there or not.

I pushed off from the top of the hill to check things more closely. It was a long time since I had made the trip down that slope, but it didn't take me long to realize my mistake. The road ran down at such a slant that my speed picked up instantly, and before I got a third of the way, I figured I was hitting seventy or eighty. I guess it really wasn't that fast, but it sure seemed like it at the time. With the wind whistling past my ears and stinging my face as I barrelled down the road, I panicked and began to squeeze the handlebars.

Then I remembered that there were no hand brakes on this old crate, and that to put on the brakes I had to pedal backwards. The pedals were whizzing around so fast that I had trouble keeping my feet on them, but I slammed them backwards as hard as I could, praying that the sudden stop wouldn't make me skid over the edge and down the bank.

There was no sudden stop. Instead the pedal and shank flew off, and I grazed my ankle painfully on the sprocket. The bike didn't even slow down. Ahead of me I could see the heavy traffic on the bypass, and I realized that if I didn't get off the road I would run straight out onto the busy highway. But there was no way I could get off Bridge Road now, because the embankment dropped sharply on each side. There seemed to be no escape from disaster.

Suddenly I recalled a flat grassy area where the bypass and Bridge Road joined. If I could steer the bike off the road there and spill at that point, I would be all right. I wondered if I'd be able to stop in time to avoid the traffic, and even considered jumping off onto the pavement, but I was still going too fast.

The bend in the road was coming up fast, and I was headed straight for the wall of the Inn. Desperately I prepared to turn the bike to the right and follow the road out to the flat area where the bank was only a few inches high.

But I hadn't reckoned on my over-inflated front tire. With a sound like a rotten tomato hitting the school wall, it burst wide open, and all of a sudden I was running on the rim, little bits of rubber flying off the wheel. Within a few seconds the wheel hit a hole in the roadway and I lost control.

Bridge Road swung right, but I didn't. Over the edge of the bank I sailed, and crashed through the hedge. Leaves flew everywhere as I slammed into the rear bumper of a car, crushing my front wheel and jamming it into the frame.

Oddly enough, I was still sitting upright on the seat, and it seemed like an eternity before I fell sideways onto the pavement, my legs tangled up in the bicycle. Leaves continued to drift down and little flashes of light popped around me.

I remember someone shouting excitedly and hands gripping my shoulders. I remember noticing green paint and seeing the licence number 5K-206. And I remember everything turning black.

'Where
are you taking me?'

I woke up lying in the back seat of a car. But even without moving my head, I could see the buildings we were passing. The steeple of the Anglican church whizzed by. We were heading north on Main Street, but where we were going I didn't know.

Cautiously I raised my head a few inches, then sank back in shock. The car I was riding in was a station wagon — a green station wagon! And at the wheel was a small, thin man with graying hair combed back from his forehead to cover a bald spot. He had hollow-looking cheeks and a kind of shadow on his face, as though he hadn't shaved for several days. I noticed deep lines on his forehead and a tightness in his jaw that made him look grim. The hands gripping the steering wheel seemed old and worn, as if they had been used to outdoor work. But he was too small and weak-looking to be a farmer or a logger. There was no doubt in my mind about who he was.

And then it began to dawn on me why I was in his car. I had been kidnapped! What would his next move be? I forced myself to calm down and concentrate.

"Where are you taking me?" I asked, glad that there was no shaking in my voice.

The man turned to glance quickly at me in the back seat. The lines on his face smoothed out and a smile, surprisingly gentle, came to his lips. His eyes were full of concern, and he wore a friendly expression.

"Just relax, son," he said. "You've had a little accident on your bicycle. I'm just taking you into the doctor's office for an examination. The first-aid fellow at the Inn said he thought you were all right, but that we'd better take you in and make sure you haven't had a concussion or something. Your bones all seem to be in order. Got any aches or pains?"

I had to think about that. There was the odd sharp pain here and there, but everything appeared to be on the surface — a few bruises, and a bit of dried blood on my knuckles and arm. The trip through the hedge had taken the knee out of my pants too, and some skin off my leg, but I was surprised to discover how healthy I had stayed in spite of the smash-up.

Before I could tell the man that I was in pretty good shape, he turned around again and gave me another of his friendly smiles. "We checked through your pockets for identification," he went on, "but there was nothing at all to help us. If you'll tell me your name and telephone number, I'll be glad to let your parents know what happened and where you are."

I was almost fooled by his smooth talk, but I caught myself in time. Here was a crook asking for my name and telephone number. Why? Not to help, I figured. He probably intended to hold me for ransom and try to get a lot of money from my father. I swallowed hard.

"I — I really can't remember," I mumbled. As blood rose in my cheeks, I was certain he would read the word "liar" on my face. He looked back at me again; the lines returned to his forehead and the smile faded.

"Don't worry about it, son," he said gently. "We'll find some way to help you." He drove on in silence, and in a few seconds we turned the corner that brought us to the doctor's office. The man turned around in his seat and stretched his arm along the back. There was a small scrap of blue paper in his hand.

"By the way," he said, "when we checked your pockets we found no identification, but we did find this. Can you tell me why you have it?"

I stared at the paper for a few seconds, suddenly feeling weaker. He was holding the bit of fertilizer bag on which I had written the licence number of his car. The charcoal lettering was very blurred, but it was still clear enough to read.

I couldn't think of any kind of answer. "I don't know," I gasped and closed my eyes, hoping it would all go away. Almost immediately, though, I had a further idea. I clutched dramatically at my chest, contorted my face as best I could and sucked in my breath. "Ohh, it hurts," I moaned.

It succeeded. The man looked at me anxiously, then jumped out of the car and ran around and opened the door beside my head. Very carefully he picked me up, and I felt myself being carried. I was worried that I might open my eyes at the wrong time, so I kept them tightly closed. I heard the man ask someone to hold the office door open, and then I was carried in. There was a flurry of activity as we entered the waiting room; next I heard a nurse say, "Bring him right in here."

The place had the same smell as when I'd last visited the doctor, the time I slammed the car door on my hand. I opened one eye in time to see the man say goodbye to the nurse. He glanced once more into the examining room where I lay, then turned and went out the front door. For such a rotten crook he seemed awfully nice, but I reminded myself that swindlers practise making people like them. At least he really hadn't kidnapped me, but he must be suspicious about the paper in my pocket, I thought.

The doctor strode in and gave me a quick check. "Well, Johnny, old boy," he said cheerfully, "looks like you'll need a few band-aids to cover your scrapes, but I don't think there's anything else to worry about. You don't seem to have any head injuries. From what the fellow said, you've gotten off pretty easily."

The nurse called my father to pick me up, and once home I was packed off to bed for rest and recovery. Scott was sternly forbidden to disturb me in any way, although he was really excited about my trip to the doctor. Cathy was banned as well, and I must admit it was a relief not to have people poking their noses around at that moment.

Mother brought me my supper on a tray, which she put on the bedside table. There was a great big slice of rhubarb pie for dessert. She smiled and then left me alone. One good thing about my mother — she didn't beat you over the head with a lot of questions if she thought you weren't feeling well. She asked them all later. For now at least I was safe.

I finished the food and lay back on the cool pillow to think over the events of the afternoon. Mother came in to collect the dirty dishes and to draw the drapes. "Try to go to sleep now, John," she said. "You'll be back to normal in the morning." The door closed silently behind her.

The room was still quite light, since the drapes were not really thick enough to shut out the late rays of sun on those July evenings. I pulled my collection of old comic books from under the bed and flipped through a couple. When I finished reading a coverless Superman comic I must have dozed off for a few minutes because the next thing I remember was opening my eyes with a start. There in front of me was Steven, standing quietly by the wall. My eyes opened wide; Steven grinned, as usual.

"Hi, John," he said cheerfully. "How are you feeling?"

"All right," I stammered. "I didn't hear you come in. What are you doing here?"

"Didn't you say I should meet you after supper? Isn't it after supper now?" He was making fun of me.

"Yes," I admitted. "But why did Mother let you in? I'm not supposed to be disturbed."

"Nobody let me in," he replied. "I just came in. Now tell me what you found out about our crook."

"The guy we're looking for is staying at the Highway Inn," I reported. "But you'll never believe what happened, Steve."

"Really?" he said. "Try me."

I went over the entire story for him, and he started to laugh. Before long he was laughing so loudly that I was afraid someone would come in to find out what was going on. But when I told him about the paper in my pocket, he stopped laughing.

"That will make him suspicious, I guess," he said. "But it can't be helped. We'll go on with the next part tomorrow or the day after, depending on when your mother will let you out of the house."

"What does the next part involve?" I asked cautiously. "Not another blast-off through the thorn bushes, I hope!"

Steven grinned at me. "Come on, John," he said. "You weren't really hurt, were you? And those weren't thorn bushes — they were lilac."

"I thought you never went across the river, Steven," I said. "How do you know they weren't thorns?" I figured I wouldn't get an answer, but this time, for some unknown reason, I did.

"Look at your shirt," he said. It was draped over the back of the chair, as I hadn't bothered to hang it up. The pocket and collar were still decorated with lilac leaves.

Steven went on with his instructions. "Listen carefully, John. Tomorrow if possible, or the next day, you have to take Cathy and Scott and investigate the houses across the river."

Take Scott! What good would he be? Cathy at least had some sense in her head, but Scott would only be in the way. I didn't say anything to Steven though.

"We have to know," he went on, "just who this crook has swindled and how much money he's taken from each of them."

"And how do we go about that?" I asked. "Just go up and ask if they paid five hundred dollars recently to have their roof fixed? People might wonder at us a little, don't you think?"

Steven was unimpressed. "You'll find some way of doing it, I'm sure," he snorted. "I did."

"What did you do?" I asked.

"The three of you can use a different method." Steven never seemed to answer the questions I thought were really important.

Familiar steps were approaching in the hallway. "Oh no," I groaned. "It's my mother! Hide, Steve, quickly!"

Immediately I turned over and hid my face in the pillow to look sound asleep. You just can't fool my mother though. When she opened the door she could tell that I hadn't been sleeping. "Was that you talking, John?" she asked.

"Uh — I'm going to sleep now. See you in the morning." She closed the door softly, and I listened to her going back down the hallway. I became aware of a faint smell of pine in the room, and figured that she had sprayed the hall with disinfectant or something.

"Okay, Steve, the coast is clear," I hissed. There was no movement or reply. "You can come out now."

There was still no answer. Steven must have hidden himself very well, because there wasn't a sign of him anywhere. I climbed out of bed and looked behind the drapes. The sunlight was still bright, but there was simply nothing there. I searched quickly through the room — in the closet, under the bed. Steven was gone.

"He must have slipped out the window," I said sleepily as I crawled back into bed. My head sank in the pillow as I murmured, ". . . and closed it behind him."

Investigating

Father got the following day off work, and after we had driven out to collect the ruins of my old bicycle from the Highway Inn, he took us all on a picnic to Rouge Creek Park. He said that Mother needed a little rest after all that baking. Everyone assumed that I had been on an innocent bike-hike when I had my accident, so there were no difficult questions to answer.

During our stay at the park, I noticed that Scott had become very friendly with Cathy. It seemed that their trip to Greenwood had been a tremendous success, and he thought she was "all right, for a girl." Cathy had entertained him while I was confined to bed, telling him strange stories and playing games. They goofed around a lot together when we were on the picnic, and I was really surprised at how she put up with him.

It was too bad I hadn't been able to find Steven. He might have come too, and we could have gone paddling in the creek or hiking along the nature trails and let

Cathy and Scott do what they wanted. I felt left out as I watched the two of them.

Before I went to bed I decided that I would get up really early the next day and start the investigation. But morning arrived long before I expected. I awoke to find that it was nine thirty and that Scott and Cathy had finished breakfast and were outside.

When I joined them, Cathy was telling Scott a rather mixed-up version of *The Legend of Sleepy Hollow.*

"And so the guy rode on his horse, Scott, faster and faster, trying to get away from the spook. He had to reach the stream and get across the bridge."

Scott piped up at this point. "How come he wanted to go across the bridge?"

"Don't you know anything about spooks?" Cathy asked in disgust. "Ghosts and spirits can't cross water. He would be safe if he crossed the stream, don't you see?" I don't think Scott really did see, but you'd never know with him anyway.

I called Cathy aside and explained what had already happened with Steven and the investigation. She was very interested. She listened carefully to everything and asked some pretty thoughtful questions, things I hadn't even worried about.

"Just how much do you know about this Steven kid?" she asked.

"Well," I confessed, "not very much, I guess, except that he lives somewhere far away from here and comes back to visit every so often. I suppose he's staying in the village with some friends or relatives. And he dresses kind of weird. But he seems like an okay kid. I trust him anyway. And he did know the crook's licence number, don't forget."

"How do you know that man is a crook?" asked Cathy. "You've only got this Steven's word for it, haven't you? You never really saw him cheat anyone, did you? And Steven didn't want to call in the police. Why not? Did you ask him for any proof?"

"No." Cathy was beginning to make me feel a little foolish. I'd never even thought that Steven might be a liar.

"Don't you want to help?" I asked lamely. Steven was going to be disappointed.

"Of course I'll help, John," she sighed. "I guess you should be able to tell as well as I can whether someone is trustworthy or not. I just wanted to know exactly what you had gotten into, that's all." It was a relief to hear her say that. I hadn't thought that I would be glad to have Cathy along on this adventure, but I was.

"Well, what do we do now?" she asked. I really hadn't the faintest idea, and Steven had been pretty unhelpful, but I rose to the occasion as best I could.

"We follow the plan," I said. "We find out who got swindled and how much money they lost. Let's go."

We didn't have any trouble persuading Scott to go with us; he was eager to set off. I still didn't see what use he would ever be, but Steven had said to take him.

The three of us walked along the river trail toward the bridge. Every so often we had to wait for Scott, who kept poking his nose into clumps of bushes or peering behind trees.

After he had done this about five times, Cathy couldn't hide her curiosity any longer. "What are you looking for, Scott? Did you lose something?"

"No," he answered. "I'm just looking for the dragon."

"What dragon?" asked Cathy. She was becoming impatient; but I knew that once Scott was off on one of these tangents, it was almost impossible to get him back on course. I was surprised that he was looking for a dragon though. I thought he was too old to believe in such things.

"You told me about the dragon," Scott said. "Remember?" He looked at Cathy eagerly.

"Oh no," she moaned, turning to me. "I told him a story yesterday, John, about a little boy who found a dragon. The dragon granted him wishes." She looked back at Scott. "You won't find any dragons here," she said, as if she were an expert on the subject. "This isn't the kind of place dragons live. Come on."

"Where do they live? Under the bridge?"

"Maybe. Let's run and see." We were then forced to charge after Scott, who made a beeline for the bridge.

There were no dragons under the bridge — just stale

damp musty air and a few pale weeds struggling to survive in the shadows. Scott was disappointed, but soon became anxious to get on with the search for dragons in other places.

In a grassy area south of the bridge a little girl about five years old was playing. She was a scruffy-looking kid, and her clothes looked as if they hadn't been washed in months. Her hair was straggly, her face streaked with dirt.

"Follow me," murmured Cathy, sounding secretive. She approached the little girl and said hello. The girl said hello back to her, then went on pulling clover flowers out of the grass.

"Do you live around here?" asked Cathy. The girl indicated a small, run-down frame house with a thick honeysuckle hedge.

"Who lives in the first house?" asked Cathy, pointing to the building beside the little girl's place.

For a few moments the girl was silent, as if thinking. "That's Mr. Kingford's house," she finally said. "You better not go there. He's mean. He calls the police if we go on his grass." I glanced up at the wide, well-kept lawn.

"Thanks," said Cathy, as she began to walk along Bridge Road. "Come on, you two. We're going to visit that green house."

"What?" I asked in amazement. "That's the place the kid was just talking about. She said the old guy that lives there is a real crab. Why do we want to go there?"

"It's part of the investigation. Steven's orders," answered Cathy. She sounded so confident that I wondered if she had also been talking to Steven and got some instructions that I had missed. Cathy was pretty good at bluffing, though, and you never could tell.

We walked through the cool tunnel of trees until we reached the gate, painted the same dark green as the trim of the house. The lawns had just been cut, and the smell of fresh grass and roses was everywhere.

"Are there any dragons here?" asked Scott.

"No," I muttered to Cathy. "Just an ogre."

She pushed open the gate and walked firmly along the path to the front door. "You two keep quiet," she whispered. "Leave the talking to me."

"You're the expert," I said.

Cathy knocked. After a long pause, an elderly man with a sour expression came to the door.

"What is it?" he demanded harshly.

"Good morning, sir," said Cathy in her most sickly-sweet voice. "I'm taking orders for Girl Guide cookies. How many boxes would you like?" She smiled shyly at him and nervously shifted her weight from one foot to the other, her hands clasped behind her back.

"What?" croaked the old man in disbelief. "What cheek! After I pay out a hundred and eighty-five dollars in property taxes to keep you in school? After I pay two hundred to the town for the blasted eavestrough repairs, and almost all the rest of my hard-earned money for Lord knows what other government foolishness, you expect me to buy your foul biscuits? Get away from here or I'll telephone the police." He slammed the door rudely in our faces.

Cathy sniffed the air and looked dignified. "They aren't foul biscuits," she said. "They happen to be delicious cookies." She stomped off down the path, and Scott and I followed, latching the gate behind us.

"What was all that about, Cathy?" I asked when we reached the road and paused for further planning. "You're not a Girl Guide. You don't have any cookies to sell."

"And you don't seem to have any brains," she said, looking at me in disgust. "What you just saw was our first success — part one of our investigation. Think about what he said, John: two hundred dollars for eavestrough repairs. Who do you suppose did those repairs, the Easter Bunny? Use your noodle, chum."

I felt my face getting hotter as I realized what she had done. I'd really have to do something clever to top the act she had just pulled off.

"Mr. Kingford, two hundred dollars," said Cathy as she marked the sum in a little black notebook she fished from her jeans pocket. If anyone deserved to be swindled out of two hundred dollars, I thought, it would be someone like the old crab we had just met.

We headed down the road, Cathy and I walking

leisurely, Scott darting from one side to the other.

I saw an elderly lady poking about in her flower garden, gathering a bunch of daisies and snapdragons. Here was my chance to equal Cathy's discovery. "Come on, you two," I urged. "And let me handle this one."

We approached the lady and stood grinning at her from our side of the fence. She smiled at us in return and pushed back her white hair with a free hand. Her face was kind and grandmotherly, and I liked her right away.

"Hello," I said. She smiled again and continued to snip off the big white daisies with her scissors. "Can I help you, ma'am?" I was really stuck for something to say, since I wasn't as quick on my feet as Cathy. Cathy looked awfully scornful.

"I don't think so, son," the lady replied. "I'm almost finished making up this bouquet. But it was kind of you to offer." She smiled at me again and turned toward the house with her flowers.

"Do you want another bunch?" I asked desperately, afraid she would escape before we found out anything. She shook her head.

"I could cut your grass," I offered. "For free."

"Mercy, you are eager to do your good deed," she said. "All right, then, you'll find the lawn mower in the shed at the back. Come and let me know when you're through." She walked into the house and left us standing at the gate.

I didn't want to look at Cathy's eyes. My plan was not running as smoothly or as easily as hers had. "Better get busy, I guess," I said, as I opened the gate and headed for the back shed. "At least my plan is working."

The lawn mower turned out to be an old muscle-power, push-type machine, and it was badly rusted. It took all my effort just to move it, but fortunately the grass was not thick under the tall trees, and it took very little time to finish. Cathy and Scott lay in the shade telling each other stories and playing guessing games. It would have been nice if one of them had volunteered to relieve me. Why did I tell them to let me handle this?

Half an hour later I knocked on the neatly-painted door of the house, not really certain what the next step in my clever plan would be. The lady took a long time answering, and I knocked again. Just then she opened the door.

"Are you finished already, young man?" she asked. "Come in for a glass of milk and some cookies, all of you." Scott and Cathy had come over from their resting place and were delighted by the invitation.

We were led into a fancy, old-fashioned living room, with white covers on all the furniture and small glass animals and potted plants everywhere. The walls and carpeting were dark and the air smelled a little musty, as if the windows were never opened. But it was a pleasant, comfortable room, though not too much light came in through the small windows.

"I don't get many visitors, you know," said the lady as she entered with a tray of milk and cookies. "You're the second I've had this week, though."

"Who else was here?" I blurted, hoping I didn't sound too nosy.

She sighed. "Only the building inspector. He's never been here before, and he found four hundred dollars' worth of damage to my foundations. Luckily, he's fixed it himself." I glanced proudly at Cathy. My discovery was twice the size of hers.

Scott was blowing bubbles in his milk again, but stopped when he noticed all of us staring at him. A new idea came into his head, and he asked the lady a question. "Are there any dragons here?"

"No, I'm afraid not," she answered. "There really is no such thing as a dragon, you know." Scott looked disappointed.

The lady went on. "I really don't know any of your names, either. Are you going to tell me, or are you like the little elves in the story about the shoemaker?" I told her my name and introduced Scott and Cathy.

The lady spent a few more minutes thanking me for cutting her grass and telling me what a good boy I was. Cathy was rather disgusted by all this, but she kept quiet.

At last we finished the milk and cookies and said goodbye. Back on the road, we stopped while Cathy

wrote in her notebook: *Lady at 84 Bridge Road, $400.*
The hill was steep at this point, and we walked a little
more slowly, except for Scott who still raced around
searching for dragons.

Opposite the "Witch's Place" we stopped and I
pointed it out to Cathy. "Lots of funny things go on in
there," I whispered.

"Like what?" Cathy asked, eying the open door and
the dark interior of the house. An empty wheelbarrow
stood half-hidden in the tall weeds in the front yard.

"Well, like the time that the — " I broke off what I
was saying. There by the fence, almost hidden by the
straggly bushes, was the witch herself. And right in front
of her, grinning from ear to ear, his eyes full of interest,
was Scott.

My heart sank even further when I heard his voice.
"Do you have any dragons?" he asked, bouncing up and
down.

"Why yes," said the witch. "Come inside and I'll
show you. Bring your friends too." She pointed at
Cathy and me.

We watched helplessly as Scott followed her up the
tangled walk to the ramshackle front porch. She
disappeared inside. "What should we do?" squeaked
Cathy.

"Come on, you guys," pleaded Scott, as he vanished
into the house.

The witch's house

"We'd better go get him, Cathy," I said. We waded through a sea of weeds toward the open door and hesitantly stepped up onto the porch. I squinted hard, trying to see what lay within. But coming out of the bright sunlight, neither of us could see a thing.

"You go first," whispered Cathy, pushing me toward the doorway. "Hurry, she might do something to Scott." I edged carefully toward the door and at last stepped inside into the gloom.

Gradually my eyes adjusted to the darkness, and I felt suddenly surprised. The cobwebs, snakes, bats, lizards, the steaming cauldron, the dust, skulls and twisted bones — everything, in fact, I had expected — were nowhere to be seen.

I found myself in a small entrance hall with a low doorway opening into a tidy living room. Scott was sitting on the edge of a battered sofa, grinning happily. The dark blue walls needed repainting, and the furniture looked old, but the room was clean. A great number of strange ornaments were scattered everywhere — on tables, shelves, ledges, the mantlepiece. The fireplace looked as if it had been used recently, since there was a thick layer of ash in the grate. The curtains might have been made of velvet, but the material was very old and the colour had streaked, the way construction paper streaks when you spill water on it. There was a threadbare carpet on the plain varnished floor.

The witch, tall and thin, appeared in the doorway and smiled at us. She was neither as old nor as ugly as I had expected. Her hair had not turned completely grey and still showed its original yellowish-brown colour, like the tops of the desks at school. Her skin was smooth and pale, not warty or speckled. But it was her eyes that impressed me most. I was sure I had seen those eyes somewhere before, but I suppose many people have the same kind of eyes. They were grey and seemed to be laughing secretly at us. She was smiling, and her face looked friendly and gentle.

"Come in, children," she urged, when she noticed us standing in the doorway. "Sit down and relax. It has grown quite warm outdoors, hasn't it? The weather is certainly changing this week. I truly do enjoy visitors, though hardly anyone ever comes any more. It gets lonely, living here by myself, and I do love to hear youngsters talking." She glanced fondly at Scott, who beamed back at her.

"We can't stay long," I said. "We have a lot of work to do this morning." I was aware of that scent of pine again and noticed a vase of pine twigs on the mantle.

The witch looked disappointed. "Surely you have time for a cup of tea," she said. "The kettle's already boiling."

Scott stared at me hopefully. "The lady has a dragon for me," he whispered. "A real dragon, John. Let's stay . . . *please*?"

The lady looked at me and winked. "It's not a real, living, fire-breathing dragon, of course," she explained. "They vanished long ago. But perhaps it will do for now." Her voice was calm and kind, and I began to wonder how people could call her a witch. Maybe it was because she believed in dragons.

I didn't try to object, and the lady went off into the kitchen. Cathy was sitting in a large armchair, looking at the ornaments on the table beside her. She picked up a photograph in a gold-coloured frame and examined it carefully. "I wonder who the kid in the picture could be," she said. "He looks something like you, John. He's got a billion freckles, anyway."

I got up to have a look at the photograph, but just then the lady came back in with a tray, and I quickly sat down again beside Scott.

She set the tray down on a small table, pushing a group of ornaments to one end, and arranged the teapot and the milk and sugar. She poured the tea and handed us each a cup, then rubbed her hands anxiously.

"I'm sorry there isn't any cake or biscuits," she said. "I'm not able to get into the town very often to shop, you know."

"Where's the dragon?" begged Scott.

"I'll get him soon," said the lady. "First tell me about yourselves."

We drank our tea as politely as we could, except for Scott who made revolting slurping sounds. We told her our names, how old we were and where we lived and went to school.

"My name is Mrs. Winch," she told us. "For some reason people around here think I'm strange. I suppose it's because the place is in such a dreadful state. My arthritis is so bad at times that I'm almost crippled, so I can't cut down the weeds or repaint the house. The inside here is as much as I can handle, and I just haven't the money to hire someone else to do the work.

"But I suppose I won't need to worry about the yard much longer," she said, with a sad little smile. Her voice sounded distant, as though she really wasn't speaking to us at all. "I'm going to have to move shortly."

"Where are you going?" asked Cathy.

"I don't know," sighed Mrs. Winch. "But I can't stay here. The house has been condemned; 'unfit to live in,' the man said."

My ears perked up. "What man?" I asked, trying not to let my excitement show through.

"The building inspector," she said simply. "He says I need almost a thousand dollars worth of repairs. I just don't have that kind of money. And at my age I can't go out and get a job, especially with my arthritis."

"That's a terrible shame," said Cathy. "But don't worry, Mrs. Winch. I'm sure something will happen to help you out." I was afraid for a moment that Cathy was going to blab everything, but she stopped there and I relaxed.

For a few minutes there was an awkward silence. Then Mrs. Winch stood up. "My goodness, Scott, I still haven't brought you the dragon, have I? You must be getting dreadfully impatient. I'll be back in a few seconds." She went off again through the kitchen.

There was a piece of silk cloth in her hand when she returned. "My husband was a sailor all our married life. He visited just about all the Pacific ports, and we lived in Vancouver for a while. Every time he returned from a voyage, he'd bring me treasures. He brought me this one year from Korea; it was the last trip he ever returned from, as a matter of fact. His ship went down in a storm on the way back to the Philippines that summer, and they never found his body."

"I'm sorry," said Cathy.

"The dragon is in here, Scott," said Mrs. Winch, laying the silk down on the sofa beside him. "You have to unfold him carefully." She began to open up the cloth. When it was laid flat, a brilliantly coloured dragon embroidered in gold, green and blue thread shone out of the fabric. It was one of the most beautiful things I have ever seen; it almost seemed alive. Scott was delighted.

"Boy, that's neat!" he gasped. "I've never seen any dragons that pretty before. What's its name, Mrs. Witch?"

Mrs. Winch seemed a little startled by the way he mixed up her name, but smiled and told him it had no name. I was terribly embarrassed by his stupid mistake.

"That dragon has waited for a long time, Scott. It has waited for a name for over thirty years now. If you can think of a good name, you can take him home with you, providing you promise to bring him back for visits every so often."

Scott was so pleased he could hardly speak, and he bounced energetically up and down on the edge of the sofa. His eyes were shining.

"Thank you! Thank you very much," he said at last. "Is it a boy dragon or a girl dragon?"

"Well, Scott," said Mrs. Winch, "I think it is probably what you want it to be. Dragons are like that, you know."

"It must be a boy dragon," Scott went on. "I have a friend at school called Patrick. I think I'll call the dragon Patrick too. Isn't that a good name?"

I didn't particularly think it was a very good name for a dragon — a Chinese name would have been better. Patrick sounded too much like a leprechaun. But Mrs.

Winch seemed to think Patrick was all right.

"That sounds fine, Scott," she said. "Would you like more tea, children? Your cups are empty."

She had already picked up the teapot, but I said, "No thanks, Mrs. Winch. We still have a lot of work to get finished before lunch." She looked very disappointed, and I hastened to add something more.

"Could I come back another time, maybe, and work in your yard for you? You wouldn't have to pay me, you know, because you've been so good to Scott."

"That's very kind of you, John," she said. "I'd really appreciate your help." Her voice quavered, and she turned around to look through an old book that was lying among the ornaments on the shelf. When she turned back and smiled at me, her eyes were wet. "Forgive me," she said. "For just a moment there, you reminded me of someone."

We walked to the door and said goodbye, thanking Mrs. Winch again for the tea and the dragon, which Scott clutched tightly in his hand.

"Have you got any more dragons, Mrs. Winch?" he asked clumsily. He at least had her name right now, but I was amazed at his greediness.

"Of course, Scott," she answered. "A great number of them. Come back another time, and you can see them."

"Oh boy!" squealed Scott. "Let's come back tomorrow, John."

I smiled sheepishly at Mrs. Winch. "He's just a little kid," I muttered. "He really doesn't mean to be rude."

"Don't worry, John," she said. "I like him just the way he is. Come back whenever you can."

Cathy and Scott were already knee-deep in the weeds.

"Oh, John," said Mrs. Winch suddenly. "Is your house far from the municipal office?"

"No," I said.

"Would you do me a favour? Could you take this paper in to the office sometime? The building inspector dropped it on the porch the other day, and I didn't notice it until he had gone." She pulled a piece of yellow paper from a small drawer and handed it to me. "It may be something important."

"I'd be glad to take it in," I said, anxious to find out what the crook had left, though not wanting to show my excitement. "It's no trouble at all, Mrs. Winch."

I said goodbye and headed toward Cathy and Scott, who were waiting for me on the road. Running through Mrs. Winch's weeds was heavy going, but I eventually reached them and raced with them down toward the bridge. Cathy kept arguing with me, saying that we still had more houses to check, but I was more interested in the yellow paper.

"Listen Cathy," I panted. "What does this sound like to you?" I began to read out loud from the crook's paper.

Kingford, 76 Bridge Road — $200.00

Ross, 84 Bridge Road — $400.00
Jason, 89 Bridge Road — $150.00
Winch, 97 Bridge Road — c.

"And there are five other names and amounts of money . . ."

"The crook's list!" shouted Cathy. "He made a list just like mine! We've found out all we need!" She skipped around in a little circle, pulling Scott by the hands. He was always ready to jump around, anywhere and with anyone.

We continued across the bridge. And there, parked alongside the playground, was the green station wagon. And guess who was standing beside it! He began to walk toward us. I froze, and Cathy stared at me.

"Hey, boy!" shouted the crook. "Come here! I want to talk to you!"

Caught!

"Hey!" called the man again. Cathy and Scott just stood staring at him.

"Come on!" I yelled, grabbing Scott's wrist and diving off the roadside into the scrub trees along the riverbank. "We've got to run!" They followed without asking any questions.

Luckily I knew my way through the willows and cedars, among the clumps of raspberry and blackberry, to the river trail. No crook would be able to move in this area as fast as I could. There was not really much chance of his finding us, but we kept on running just the same until we were nearly home. We stopped briefly to catch our breath.

"Cathy," I panted, "would you take Scott home? I'll see if I can find Steven anywhere. Show Mother your dragon, Scott, and tell her about your visit with Mrs. Winch."

"What about the crook?" asked Cathy. "Won't he

still be around here in the bushes?" She looked a little frightened even then.

"I'll be really careful, Cathy," I promised. "Don't worry about me."

She agreed unwillingly. "Well, all right then. Do you want me to come back after I've taken Scott home?"

"Mother won't let you," I said. "It's lunch time. Tell her I'll only be a few minutes longer."

Cathy and Scott headed off through the trees toward home, and I began to wander about trying to think of a way of getting in touch with Steven. I knew he sometimes came down by the river, but I had no idea when he might show up. I also didn't know where he was staying in the village.

I waited as long as I could, but there was no sign of my friend. I went home for lunch.

Scott had the silk dragon spread out on the kitchen floor and was stroking it as if it were a live puppy. Mother had to walk carefully around him as she tried to get lunch on the table. Cathy had already told her that Scott's story about getting the silk was true, but Mother still suspected Scott of mixing up, as usual, what really happened.

"Mrs. Winch has lots more dragons!" Scott went on excitedly. "We can go back and see another one tomorrow, can't we, John?"

I nodded. Cathy wandered back into the kitchen and picked up the silk cloth.

Scott was still talking. "I hope that man doesn't come tomorrow, though, John." I tried desperately to shush him up, but he added, "I didn't like him. Especially when he was chasing us in the woods."

I knew Mother would not ignore this news. "What man, Scott? Who chased you?" she asked.

"You got us into this, Scott," I said to myself. "Now I hope you can get us out of it." Instead, he dragged us all farther in.

"A man in the road," explained Scott. "He was trying to catch John, but we ran away and hid in the trees, and he couldn't find us anywhere 'cause we were too far away."

Mother looked hard at me. "Why did he want to catch you, John? What had you been doing?"

"Nothing, honest," I protested. "We didn't even say anything to him. We were just walking home from Mrs. Winch's house, weren't we, Cathy?"

"That's right," Cathy said.

Mother stared into our faces, and we tried to look as innocent as possible. She claimed she could always tell by my face whether I was telling the truth, and I hoped my freckles were all in order.

"If that's the case, maybe we'd better call the police. Men who chase children in the street without reason sound pretty dangerous to me."

"Maybe he had a reason," Cathy said quickly, trying frantically to think of one. She found it, but it didn't

67

sound very convincing. "Maybe he thought he knew us. We were too scared to stop and find out."

I knew that Mother would hate to trouble someone who really was innocent, and I kept my fingers crossed.

"Well," she said, "I'm glad you didn't stop, even if he did know you. I still don't know whether to call the police . . ."

We waited anxiously to see what her decision would be, but she never announced it. She just went on with lunch and soon we were eating.

"What were you planning to do this afternoon?" asked Mother as we finished our dessert.

"I think I'll teach Scott how to play fish," said Cathy.

Scott looked at her in disgust. "I already know how to play fish," he said. "Do you want me to teach you how to play cribbage?" I had played cribbage with Scott and was about to warn Cathy, when they became involved in a big discussion over who knew the most card games and who was better at what.

Mother shrugged her shoulders. "Maybe the dragon will swallow them both," she said. "What are you planning to do, John?"

"I want to go and meet this friend of mine, Steven. Then maybe I'll go crayfish hunting at the shallows." A worried look came into Mother's eyes. "Don't look at me like that," I said. "I'm always really careful around the river. It's shallow, and you know I'm a good swimmer. I won't drown."

I could never really decide whether she was more concerned about my drowning or about the crayfish that I sometimes brought home. Once I left a bucket of them in the basement to study for a few days before dumping them back into the river. I completely forgot about them and went off with the family on vacation. We came back to a house that smelled like rotten fish for weeks.

But Mother was no longer thinking about crayfish. She had another idea. "Before you go, John, would you please pick all the red currants from the back? Here's a bowl." I'm not very fond of picking currants, but the red ones are easier than the black ones, and currants easier than gooseberries, since there are no thorns to worry about. To Mother's surprise I took the bowl and went right out to the back garden to work. The chore was finished sooner than either Mother or I had expected, which was pleasant. Then I set off toward the shallows, hoping to run into Steven somewhere.

As I left, Scott and Cathy were sitting on the front porch madly playing cards. Scott tended to change the rules of the game if he was losing, and was used to getting away with it. Cathy didn't like the way he played, thinking that little kids should be taught to play fair. She had called him a cheater, which made him angry, and the argument was getting violent as I came by.

"It's best to humour him," I whispered to Cathy, but she didn't seem to want my advice.

As I cut through the field, I could still hear them arguing. Why doesn't Mother get after them? I thought.

The woods were cool, and the river trail was dark and damp and smelled of cedar. The birds remained strangely quiet, as though waiting for something.

Steven was standing in the path about halfway to the shallows. His grey eyes shone eagerly, and he looked ready to break out into his usual grin. Across his face and nose the freckles seemed to be rearranging themselves all the time, the way everyone says mine do when I'm excited about something. He was still wearing the same clothes he had worn when I first met him two days before.

"Any news, John?" he asked politely, but I could feel the eagerness in his voice.

"Oh, not really," I said. He looked disappointed. "Just a list of nine places where the crook tried to cheat people out of their money. He succeeded in eight of them."

Steven looked pleased. "What's the total amount, John?"

To tell the truth, I had been expecting him to tell me how wonderful my discovery was and what a smart detective I'd been. The question about amounts caught me off guard.

"Oh," I said foolishly, "I haven't bothered to check

the total. Just a moment and I'll add it up. Two hundred, six hundred, seven fifty, eleven hundred . . ." I did the rest silently, so he couldn't hear how slowly I added. Arithmetic wasn't my strong point.

"Two thousand, five hundred," I announced at last. "Want me to check it again?"

"No, that's great, John. He's gotten three thousand on this side of the river, so altogether that makes fifty-five hundred dollars. I think the crook was finishing off over here just this morning, so he'll be ready to leave for a new location. He may relax for a few days, but he'll probably leave town to do it. We'd better get on with the next part of the plan."

I had a vague feeling that the next part of the plan would involve more work for me. "Explain the next part," I sighed.

"Well, John," he said, "all you have to do is slip into his room at the Highway Inn and get the money back. Don't worry about anything else for now."

"Oh!" I exclaimed. "Is that all? I thought maybe you wanted me to do something difficult. Should I go blindfolded to make it more of a challenge?"

"Smart alec," said Steven with a grin. "Don't you want to go through with it?"

I suppose he knew all along how keen I was. "Of course I'll go through with it," I insisted. I had been to the Inn when it opened and still had a fairly good idea of where everything was, but the whole plan scared me a little. I couldn't let Steven know that, though.

"It may take me a while to get an idea," I said, adding under my breath, "and to work up the nerve."

"Don't take too long," Steven warned. "We haven't much time." He turned and walked away toward the road, and I again felt myself inhaling the scent of pine.

He must carry pine cones in his pockets, I thought. I half expected him to disappear when he reached the sunlit area beyond the edge of the woods, but he walked across the field and passed along the street until he went out of sight among the houses.

I continued on my way to the shallows, wondering how on earth I could break into a motel room, find the money and get out again without being caught.

I had thought up and thrown out at least four plans, when I froze in my tracks. The trail passed close to the street, and I could see the pavement through the thin wall of trees. There, walking toward me along the shoulder of the road, in greyish-brown shorts and a green shirt, was the crook. He was dragging a protesting little boy, younger than me, by the hand. *That boy is being kidnapped*! flashed through my mind. *What can I do to save him*?

There was no time to consider things carefully, and all I could come up with was Cathy's famous "leap from ambush." My only chance was to surprise him long enough for the kid to escape and then get away myself. Quickly I sneaked back through the scrub willow until I was well ahead of them, then waited breathlessly in the tall grass. I could see that the boy was no longer struggling, so the crook would be off his guard. Closer and closer they came; as I crouched down farther in my hiding spot, their feet passed only a couple of yards away. Hopefully the kid would be alert enough to run when I made my move. I certainly wasn't going to get a second chance to save him.

A split second later I leaped from the grass and landed on the crook's back, uttering the most blood-curdling scream I could manage. Instantly he let go of the boy.

"Run, kid, run!" I shrieked, but the boy didn't move. He just began screeching himself.

The crook lurched sharply, and I fell from his back. I scrambled to make my escape, but he was faster than I expected. Before I could get up again, he had grabbed my arms and pulled me to my feet. For such a puny guy, he was awfully strong.

He glared fiercely at me, his eyes filled with anger and his mouth twisted in rage. His grip tightened on my arms until they began to hurt.

"Now, kid," he muttered, "you've got a few things to explain."

Cathy to the rescue

The man shook me roughly, but I remained speechless. My heart was pounding wildly.

"Speak up, boy," he growled through clenched teeth.

"What — what do you mean?" I asked, tears streaming down my face.

"First you ram into my car with your bike. For some unknown reason, you have my licence number in your pocket. Then you run like mad when I call you in the street. And now you fly out of the bushes like a madman and attack me. What's going on?" He rattled me again, until I was afraid my arms would break.

"I — I don't know," I gulped, choking on the words.

"Stop bawling!" he ordered harshly. "Maybe I can refresh your memory for you — " He didn't finish what he was going to say. Suddenly he yelped and let go of my arms.

Without waiting for more encouragement, I bolted for the safety of the woods. I had forgotten all about the little boy. If he was too dumb to run, that was his tough luck now.

I knew the woods perfectly and headed for the thickest part. Not until I reached the blackberry patch near the shallows did I stop running. Still panting for breath and shaking all over, I dropped to my hands and knees and crawled into the thicket along my secret scratch-free pathway. I doubted I could be found; but even if I was, I felt I'd be able to outmanoeuvre the crook with no trouble. When I reached the end of the pathway and found the fern-leaf nests that Graham and I had made, I was still considering emergency plans.

The nests were in fairly good shape; nobody had been there since we had made them. The dried fern was soft, and it crunched a little when I lay in it. The nests had a pleasant smell, like hay, and the blackberries inter-twined overhead to shut out the sky. I stretched out and breathed deeply, trying to stop the shaking in my fingers. The smooth rustle of the river in its stony bed and the soft buzz of insects in the blackberries were the only sounds I heard as I stared out at the deep shadowy patches made by the tall trees.

As I began to unwind, my eyes closed. But suddenly I jolted upright. What was that rustling noise? Someone was creeping into the blackberry patch along my secret pathway! The little hairs on the back of my neck stood up, and I shivered.

As quietly as I could, I got ready to make a wild dash

through the bushes to the shallows and then on to the thick hedges across the river.

"Hey, John!" said a familiar voice.

"In here," I breathed. "Gosh, Cathy, you scared the wits out of me. What are you doing?"

"Rescuing you, you nitwit," she said disgustedly. "Been searching these woods for an hour to find you!"

"Huh?"

"That Scott is a terrible cheat. I just got sick of playing cards with him and decided to find you. Boy, what a shock when I did. I saw you jump that guy, and then I saw him grab you. I just had to help."

"What did you do?"

"I looked around for something to heave at him, but I was afraid to use a stone in case I really hurt him. There was a rotten old orange that someone had chucked away. I hated to even touch it, but I picked it up and threw it at him anyway. I'll bet he was surprised when that burst all over the back of his head!"

"Gosh, he wasn't half as surprised as I was, Cathy. You saved my life." She smiled modestly. "Where did the man go after I got away?"

"He took that boy and went back to town, I guess," Cathy replied. "Are you coming home? Or do you plan to get into another jam?"

"No way! Let's go and hunt crayfish." Cathy didn't look very keen, so I offered instead to show her the shallow path across the river. "You can walk across without getting your knees wet," I said. She decided to try it.

"Watch out for the dark areas in the water," I warned her. "That means it's pretty deep there, and you might slip in over your head."

"I can swim perfectly well," she sniffed.

We pulled off our shoes and socks and waded in.

"Under all these big stones are crayfish," I pointed out. As Cathy looked uneasy, I hastened to reassure her. "But they won't come out unless you lift the rocks."

"Let's not," she said.

The water flowed quickly over the flat stones, cooling our feet as it swirled around our ankles. Carefully we picked our way along the shallow path, until at last we reached the gravel bar that split the stream in two. "This is the halfway mark," I announced. "Sometimes you can find things washed up here — " I didn't finish.

"Duck!" I yelled, and pushed Cathy off the bar into a deep pothole. I jumped in after her, and while we were treading water, I tried to clamp my hand over her mouth. For a moment she thrashed, then bit my hand.

It was all I could do to keep from crying out in pain myself. Cathy found a footing and stood with the water up to her chin, her long hair clinging to her face. She glared at me. "What's wrong? Why did you push me?"

"Keep low for a minute and wait for the signal," I ordered. Cathy realized it wasn't a joke and did as she was told. We waited in the cold water.

"Now head for the shore, quickly!" We climbed out of the well and scrambled across the river to the blackberry hideout. By the time we reached the nests, we were panting for breath as well as soaked to the skin. I had a bruised ankle.

"Okay, John," demanded Cathy. "What gives? If you did all that to try to scare me, I'll drag you through these blackberry bushes until you come out shredded." She wasn't kidding.

"Didn't you notice?" I almost shouted. "There we were, standing in full view on that gravel bar, and the crook drove over the bridge in his green station wagon."

"Whew!" she sighed. "I'm glad it was him."

"How come?" Her reply didn't make much sense to me.

"Because I'm too tired to drag you through all these bushes, you idiot." She grinned. I grinned back and suddenly began to laugh at her sitting in the nest with bits of dried fern clinging to her clothes and hair, everything sopping wet and stringy-looking.

Cathy sneered. "You're pretty scruffy looking yourself, you know. You'd better go get our shoes and socks. After all, the crook might come back and steal them or throw them in the water."

When we had our shoes and socks back on our feet, we set out wearily for home, trying to think up ways of explaining our wetness to Mother.

"I think it would be best to tell the truth," I

suggested at last. "That I pushed you into a well and then jumped in myself. I could say it was a joke, and you could say it didn't bother you. I'll probably have to stay in my room, though. That means I won't be able to help Steven."

"Oh, we'll find some way around it," she said.

We left the river trail and stepped into the deep grass in the field beside my house. Suddenly we stopped short, and I forgot all about such little things as having to stay in my room.

There, parked right in our driveway, was a police cruiser. A policeman was standing beside it, talking with Mother and Scott. Cathy and I looked at each other, our faces pale with fright.

"What do you think he wants?" asked Cathy.

"I don't know," I said. "But we have to go over now. He's seen us already." Scott was staring hard at us as we crossed the field, and by the time we reached the driveway everyone's eyes were on us.

"This must be the boy we've been waiting for," said the policeman.

Shadow at the window

I stood there miserable in my wet clothes, waiting for the handcuffs and the trip to prison that I was sure would follow. Mother was still staring at me with a shocked expression on her face, and a subdued Scott was peering out from behind her.

At last someone spoke.

"What happened, John?" asked Mother. "How did you get all wet? And Cathy, you're soaked too."

"I'm sorry," I said sadly.

"We were in the river," added Cathy. "Crossing the shallow part." There was no confidence in her voice as she spoke. Both of us stood looking dismally at our shoes, which were now also soaked, thanks to the water dripping off our clothes.

"Well, John," said the policeman, "we've received a report about you, my boy."

"I know," I sighed with a hollow voice.

"It's from a Mrs. Ross, a widow. She lives over on

Bridge Road. She says you volunteered to cut her grass, and then refused to accept any money."

"I know," I repeated. "It's all my fault." Cathy kicked me in the ankle.

The policeman seemed a little surprised by this reply, but he continued. "I'm glad to hear that, John." He smiled at me. "The *Village Weekly* would like to do a story about you."

"What do you mean?" I was beginning to realize that I was not being arrested.

"As you perhaps know, we've been having a lot of trouble here lately with hoodlums. They've attacked younger children, smashed windows, torn down the fence in front of the municipal office and behaved rowdily in the streets. And the signs are that things are getting worse."

"Worse?" asked Mother.

"Yes, I'm afraid so. Just this afternoon we received a report that a gang of delinquents attacked a man walking along River Street with his little boy. They didn't hurt the boy, fortunately, and the man wasn't injured either, but he was certainly shaken up. It's the first time these hoodlums have attacked an adult, and it was in broad daylight. The community certainly gets a bad name from these kids, and the man was a stranger staying out at the Highway Inn."

"I hope he managed to give you a description of the boys who attacked him," said Mother.

I hope he didn't, I thought to myself.

"Yes," said the policeman, "he did tell us what one boy looked like and we'll try our best to find him, but we really haven't too much hope. The man was very reluctant to tell us his own name and address, and didn't seem to like dealing with us at all. He's anxious to leave town, I suppose, and doesn't want to be called back as a witness in a court case. If people won't back us up, though, it makes our job extremely difficult."

"That's too bad," Mother replied. "Imagine that kind of thing happening right here on our street. I hope the children will be safe. I haven't exactly been keeping them in the house." She looked worried.

"At any rate," said the policeman, "let's get back to the reason for my visit. Part of my job on the force is to talk to school children about safety and so on and to write the police column for the *Village Weekly*. The *Weekly* is not very happy about having only bad news to publish about the activities of our local young people. They asked if I would write about some kids who are spending their summer usefully, or taking time to think about others. When Mrs. Ross telephoned about John, we thought he sounded like an ideal subject. The story of his kindness to Mrs. Ross would certainly balance some of the bad publicity our kids have been getting lately. It might even influence a few others in deciding how to spend their summer vacation. It's too bad we don't have more like John, instead of those young punks who jumped that man on River Street."

Mother nodded doubtfully, but then smiled proudly at me.

"So, John, shall I write up your story for my column in the paper? We'll take a picture of you too."

I looked around at the others. Mother, Scott and the policeman were smiling at me expectantly. I glanced at Cathy, but she turned her head away quickly. Fat lot of help you are, I thought. Then I made up my mind.

"There must be lots of kids who do better things than what I did," I said. "I really don't deserve anything special." I was worried about having my picture in the paper right then, since the man at the Inn might recognize me. Coupled with the story about Mrs. Ross, it wouldn't take too much thinking to figure out what I was up to.

"But I think you do deserve something special," urged the policeman. "I wouldn't have come around here if I didn't."

"I'm sorry," I repeated firmly. "I don't want any story in the newspaper."

"I'm sorry to hear that John," said the policeman. "But of course I'll respect your decision." He nodded to Mother and began to get back into the cruiser.

"Keep up the good work," he called as he pulled the cruiser door shut. "And let me know if you change your mind."

"I will," I promised, as the engine started.

We watched the car pull out of the driveway. Mother put her hands on my shoulders. "I'm very proud of you, John," she said, "even if you do fall into the river."

Cathy and I went to our rooms to change into dry clothing, and then I continued on out to the back garden. After searching the house, Cathy found me outside and launched her attack.

"Oh, John," she began, "I thought I was going to explode! That poor policeman! If only he knew, eh?"

"You aren't very funny," I groaned.

Cathy had to stop teasing me because she was called off to help prepare dinner, but my "good deed" was the talk of the supper table that evening, with the whole situation reviewed for my father. Cathy kept looking at me and giggling, and for once I could hardly wait to get to bed, if only to cut myself off from talk of my "generous actions."

It was a cool evening, and I dozed off before it got dark. The afternoon's events — and the good scare I'd got — had tired me out even more than the lawn mowing.

Once asleep, I found myself dreaming of my meeting with the crook. In my dream I jumped onto the crook's back and was pulled off, just as I had been in the afternoon. But this time Cathy didn't rescue me. Desperately I managed to twist free and run for safety, but the crook followed me. I felt myself straining to escape and getting no farther ahead, no matter how hard

I tried. At last I spotted my house. Rushing up onto the porch, I bolted in through the front door, locked it and ran into my bedroom. I dived into bed, pulling the covers over my head, waiting expectantly. I could hear the crook pounding on the front door, and then all was quiet until I heard him try the window catch. Somehow I knew that the window was unlocked and felt chilled with fear — so much so that I woke up and lay in the dark, breathing heavily and shivering every few moments.

Then, unexpectedly, I really did hear something scrape across the screen on the window. I jerked my head around with a start. The drapes were drawn and there was no moon, so all was in darkness. Another soft scrape at the window broke the stillness.

At that instant a car turned the corner onto River Street, and the headlights cast the shadow of the window frame onto the drapes. I watched in horror as something else was projected on the drapes — the shadow of a long, thin, bony hand.

It was too much. I yelled at the top of my lungs, long and hard. The hand jerked back from the window before the shadow disappeared.

Father came rushing into the room and flashed on the lights. "What's wrong, John?" he asked anxiously.

I covered my eyes against the sudden brightness of the light. "A man was trying to get in the window," I panted. "A little, thin man." Before I had finished my explanation, Mother and Cathy appeared and soon Scott, still rubbing sleep from his eyes, drifted in as well.

Father opened the window and peered out into the blackness. "There's no one out there, John," he said. "You were probably having a bad dream."

"No," I insisted. "There really was someone there. I saw his shadow and even heard the noises he was making. I was awake."

"Well, whoever it was has gone now. Why don't you go and sleep with Scott for the rest of the night? Take your pillow with you." I needed no more encouragement. After all, Scott's bedroom was closer to my parents'.

As I crawled into bed with Scott, Mother turned out the light. I had been determined to lie awake and catch the crook if he tried to break in again, but the next thing I remember was the smell of bacon.

When I came into the kitchen, I found Scott dressed and already finished breakfast. "Can we go and see the dragon house today?" he pleaded.

"We'll see," I mumbled. I really wasn't entirely awake and was reluctant to commit myself to anything before I could think clearly. "Where's Cathy?" I asked.

"Still asleep. I think she spent the night listening for burglars," laughed Mother. "Do you remember your nightmare last night?"

I snorted and dropped another slice of bread into the

toaster. "Can I have some of this juice?"

Scott was lying on his back on the floor, pushing himself along with his feet and making noises to show that he was now a motorboat.

"We'll go and see Mrs. Winch this morning, Scott," I promised. "I told her we'd help clean up her yard. Go and see if Cathy wants to come, will you?"

Cathy did want to go but of course she couldn't leave until she had dressed and had her breakfast. I went out in the yard to wait.

I had just pulled off a wide blade of grass to make a reed whistle when to my surprise I saw Steven coming toward me. He plunked himself down and grinned his usual greeting.

"Boy, am I glad to see you," I exclaimed. I told him about everything that had happened the day before, about my dream and the man at the window. Steven just laughed at my predicament, then became very serious.

"We'll have to act soon, John," he said. "I think the crook will leave either tomorrow or the following day. I checked yesterday afternoon on what he was doing, and he plans to make two more 'inspections' this morning. I don't suppose he'll want to hang around much longer, especially if you've been throwing rotten oranges at him. He's probably more than a little suspicious right now."

"I'll try and think of a way to get the money, Steve.

But it will have to be this afternoon. I promised Scott I'd take him someplace this morning." I noticed that my running shoe was undone and bent down to tie it. "Will this afternoon be soon enough?" There were pine needles caught in the laces, and I pulled them out. But there was no answer from Steven. I looked up to find myself once again alone in the back yard.

Not for long though. Scott and Cathy came pounding through the back door into the yard. Scott did a few rolls on the grass just for practice.

"Let's go, slowpoke," shouted Cathy.

"Look who's talking!" I retorted. "Hey, wait a second, I want to check on something." I went over to my bedroom window and examined the ground beside the house. There were markings in the soft earth.

"Find any mysterious footprints?" called Cathy.

"No," I said truthfully. There was nothing mysterious about those footprints. I'd have recognized them anywhere. They were made by a raccoon.

"We're off to see Mrs. Winch," I cried, grabbing Scott's arm and pulling him toward the field.

Dragons
and more dragons

When we reached Mrs. Winch's house, Scott jumped up on the porch, ignoring the steps, and pounded heavily on the front door with his fist.

"Take it easy," said Cathy. "Leave the house standing."

Mrs. Winch seemed surprised by our visit, but she greeted us cheerfully and invited us in.

"We didn't come for tea this morning, Mrs. Winch," I said.

"No," agreed Scott. "We came to see the dragon."

"Don't pay any attention to him," I interrupted. "We came to help you with your yard. You tell us what to do and we'll do it. Fair enough?"

Mrs. Winch was reluctant at first to let us work. "I'm just an old lady," she said. "You must have much more interesting things to do this morning." I began to wonder if she was trying to get rid of us; but I kept on offering and finally Mrs. Winch gave us something to do.

"Do you think she was hoping we'd go home?" asked Cathy, struggling with a big dandelion. "She sure didn't want us to work here."

"I don't think it's that," I said. "I think she was afraid we really didn't want to do it. She sure was smiling when she saw we meant it."

"Yes, I guess you're right. She's probably too proud to admit that she needs help. Ouch! Thistles sure can stab you, can't they?"

Scott was racing from one end of the yard to the other, collecting buttercups. Cathy and I felt he wasn't being too helpful, but at least he was staying out of the way.

The morning wore on faster than we realized, and Mrs. Winch called us in for tea. As we surveyed our work from the porch, we decided it really looked much the same as when we'd started. Scott gave the buttercups to Mrs. Winch, who placed them in a jar in the kitchen.

"My goodness, children," she said. "You've done a wonderful job on the yard. And you've been working for more than an hour. I'm so pleased with you." She smiled at us, and again I felt that her eyes were somehow familiar.

"Can we see the dragon now?" asked Scott as he settled into his spot on the sofa. "My mother really liked that other one, you know."

The old lady laughed. "Of course, Scott. This one is

rather special too, but in a different way. It can sting."

Scott bounced up and down on the sofa while Mrs. Winch fussed with the tea tray and passed the cups around.

"Now, children," she said, "enjoy your tea while I find the dragon." She vanished through the kitchen doorway. Scott was so excited that he almost spilled his tea on his lap.

She came back into the living room carrying a black stick about a foot and half long. "Here we are. The dragon with the sting. See him carved into the wood?"

She handed the stick to Scott. It was carved in the shape of a long, thin dragon, coiled round and round. There were flowers and leaves and what looked like Chinese words scattered among the dragon's folds, and the black wood had been polished until it glistened.

"Before you hurt yourselves, though," warned Mrs. Winch, "I'd better show you a few things about this stinging dragon. Do you see these names in Chinese?" She indicated the characters along the length of the dragon's body.

"Each of them stands for a different disease. Watch how I open the stick." She pushed on the stick where one of the characters was written, and it popped open to reveal a set of large silver needles.

"Wow!" I said. "That looks dangerous."

"On the contrary," said Mrs. Winch. "The Chinese believe they can cure diseases by using these needles."

"Like the needles we get at school," said Cathy.

"Oh no, not like those, Cathy. These needles are used in what is called acupuncture. Doctors think that by sticking needles into certain parts of the body and leaving them there for a while, they can treat whatever disease a person has. The needles are solid silver, and I think they are supposed to have magical powers. There are lots of them in this dragon-case, see?" She closed the first compartment and opened another, then a third, so we could see the different sized needles.

"Now, Scott, look at the dragon's tooth." She pulled off one end of the stick to reveal a great big silver needle, about six inches long.

"Wow!" said Scott in amazement. "I wouldn't want him to bite *me*!"

"He won't if you handle him carefully. This case came from the old court of Imperial China. The Chinese believed that dragons were good creatures, always ready to help people. During the Chinese Revolution in the early nineteen-hundreds, it fell into someone else's hands, and Mr. Winch bought it in Hong Kong. This was a very special gift."

"It sure is neat," said Scott.

"Would you like to take it home to show your mother and father?" asked Mrs. Winch.

"Oh boy! Can I?" Mrs. Winch nodded, and Scott clutched the stick so firmly I was afraid it might break. "Be careful not to lose any of the needles, though.

Don't open any of the little doors while you're outside."

Scott promised to guard it with his life if necessary.

"I suppose we'd better go home for lunch now," I said. "Should we come back this afternoon and finish off the yard?"

Mrs. Winch looked at me with a strangely unhappy expression, then answered. "Not this afternoon, John. I have to go into town. My arthritis has been much less painful today, and I must go while I am able."

"Would you like us to go for you?" asked Cathy.

"No, that would not work," said Mrs. Winch with a faraway look on her face. "I must go myself." Her voice trailed off and we were afraid to say anything more.

"It was very kind of Scott to pick the pretty yellow flowers," she added after a long pause. "I wonder if I could ask you to get me some green branches or leaves to go with them before you return home for lunch?"

Scott and I went outside to get the leaves and came back in with a handful of the soft green twigs from the lower branches of the pine tree in the front yard.

"Ah," sighed Mrs. Winch. "I love pine. It always makes me feel so comfortable. Thank you, Scott. Thank you, John."

She went into the kitchen to put the pine in with the buttercups.

"Have you got any more dragons?" asked Scott, before I could silence him.

94

Mrs. Winch came back into the doorway. "Yes, Scott, I do. If you ask your mother and father, perhaps you can come back after dark some night to see them." Scott swung his arms around in excitement, and Cathy and I were afraid he might knock some of the ornaments off the table before he calmed down again.

"We really have to go now," I said, and Mrs. Winch saw us to the door and waved goodbye as we went down Bridge Road toward the river. Scott was carrying the dragon stick as though it would crumble if he looked at it the wrong way. He'd never been more careful.

Mother exclaimed over the delicate carving of the stick, and it was the major topic of conversation at lunch. But Cathy and I had to do the dishes, and Scott was sent off to clean up his room before we were allowed back outside.

I wanted to see if Steven had any more news about the crook, but Cathy and Scott said they were too tired from all they had done that morning. It was unusual for Scott to admit to being tired for any reason, but he decided to stay home and play cards with Cathy.

I was always glad to leave the open field and let myself sink into the cool shadow of the woods, especially on warm days like that one. The dense cedar scrub that faced our house was almost like a barricade, protecting the dim interior from the sun. I stopped for a moment and breathed in the damp air. It wasn't cedar I smelled — it was pine.

"Steven," I called softly.

Steven pushed his way through the bushes and stood with me in the small clearing under the trees. "Hi, John," he said.

"Want to go over our plans for getting the money?" I asked.

Steven seemed worried and anxious to be gone. "Not right now, John. I — I have to, uh, go someplace. It's really important. I'll see you tomorrow, all right?"

"But the money — " I began. Steven was already walking away through the bushes. "Not this time, you don't," I muttered. I decided to follow him and find out just where he went.

But following Steven was not as easy as I had expected. The sunlight falling through the treetops made yellow patches on the trunks, and the shadows themselves seemed to move. Many times I thought for a moment that a patch of sunlight was Steven's head, or that a dark shadow under the dense cedar was his blue pants.

We went along the river trail, and I waited in a hiding spot while he climbed up the small gravel bank from the woods to Bridge Road, then cut across the playground. I didn't want to come out of the woods until I was sure that Steven wouldn't see me. He's probably going to have a swing or something before he goes home, I thought to myself.

But Steven didn't stop at the swings. And he didn't

head into town. Instead, he continued on into the woods behind the playground.

I rushed up to the pavement and crossed quickly through the playground before he would have time to get far into the woods. I had been to that area once or twice when I was a lot younger, though I wasn't at home there as I was in the bush along the river.

But when I reached the trees Steven was nowhere in sight. The ground was higher here than near the river, and the woods were mainly maple and beech. Countless seedlings blocked my line of vision in every direction.

"Darn it," I muttered. There was no clue in the still leaves, no breath of sound to follow.

I decided to go straight ahead and at least find out how big the woods were. I had never gone more than a few hundred feet into them before.

The seedlings made the way difficult in places, but the ground was mostly free of fallen logs. A few of the forlorn-looking daisies that grow in shaded places pushed their heads up among the old leaves.

I had penetrated a fair distance into the woods before I began to wonder if I could find my way back. I was just ready to give up my search and go home when I saw a wire fence stretching off to both left and right ahead of me. Beyond the fence the trees thinned out, and the brightness showed that there was a cleared area.

I went on and climbed over the fence. Steven was probably in the clearing, I thought, maybe meeting someone. I decided to move cautiously until I found out what was happening.

The cleared area was a lawn, dotted with trees and well-kept shrubs. It took me a few minutes to recognize the place — I'd been there several times before. Beyond a hedge were the headstones of the cemetery. The part where I was standing was not yet being used.

I moved behind the bushes and tried to get in closer to the main part of the graveyard. I was just about to congratulate myself on my sneakiness, when I was startled to see someone standing quite near to me.

The grave had no headstone and was decorated only by a glass jar filled with buttercups and pine branches. The smell of pine was almost overpowering here, although the trees were all maples and willows.

I recognized the woman standing with her back to me. But what was Mrs. Winch doing at the cemetery? Her husband was dead, but hadn't she said something about his drowning and not being found?

Mrs. Winch bent over to arrange the buttercups and the pine branches. As she did so, I began to recall all the old stories about Mrs. Winch hanging around the cemetery. Some kids said she stayed there all night. Maybe she really was a witch.

"No way," I said to myself. "It's probably her mother's grave or something."

Mrs. Winch stood up, and I ducked down behind the bushes, feeling awfully guilty about spying on her. As

she turned, I could see that she had been crying. Then she ran her hand across her eyes and began to limp across the lawn toward the road. I sat in the bushes, watching her get farther and farther away.

That pine sure stinks, I thought, as I too got up and headed for home.

The search

I didn't know whether we should visit Mrs. Winch after dark that night, but both Cathy and Scott were anxious to go, and Mother said we could if we didn't stay too late. She wasn't worried about bedtime for Cathy or me, but Scott had to have enough sleep or he would get crabby.

I hadn't told the others about my spying on Mrs. Winch that afternoon, so I was the only one who knew where she had been. All the old stories I had heard returned to me — how she stayed for hours at the cemetery, waiting for something; how she called up spirits; how she stared at the sky. And a creepy, eerie feeling came over me.

But that was all nonsense. I knew Mrs. Winch — there was no way she could be evil. Yet I still wondered about her trip to the graveyard.

When we reached her house, we stopped in surprise. It really did look weird after dark. Sparks were darting out the chimney, some of them travelling high enough to set the trees on fire. It reminded me of the fireworks I had seen last Victoria Day. The door was open, and there was a strange smoke or vapour coming from within. Although no lights seemed to be on, a dull glow lit up the gaping doorway. I wasn't in any hurry to go in.

But Scott started leaping around like an idiot and pulling on my arm. "Look, John! Sparks! Smoke! Wow, there must be a real dragon in there this time!"

Cathy was interested in the sparks for a different reason. "That could cause a fire," she said. "We had one in our chimney last year, because it hadn't been cleaned for a long time and sparks started burning."

Scott, as usual, was first inside. He didn't even bother knocking this time, but Mrs. Winch didn't seem to mind. She greeted us cheerfully and led us into the living room. The fireplace was blazing, although the weather was warm.

"Are you ready for the dragons, children?" she asked.

Scott nodded his head violently up and down.

"These dragons will be harder to see, though," warned Mrs. Winch, as she picked up a box filled with numerous tiny jars from a nearby table. She knelt down in front of the fireplace.

"I shouldn't really get down like this." She laughed. "It might be impossible for me to get back up." She set the box beside her and removed one jar. "Watch closely,

102

now, and concentrate on the fire. You will have to use your imaginations, and the dragons only appear for a few seconds. Look for their eyes and the tall scales on their backs. You will see them coiling around like snakes." She tipped something from the jar into her hand and threw it onto the flames.

Instantly the flames formed a streaked greenish pattern, and the green parts coiled and twisted. As I watched, I thought I saw dragon shapes in the fire, but of course it was just my imagination. Mrs. Winch had another of the bottles in her hand, and we kept staring in fascination as she tossed more powder in the grate. The green flames were slowly replaced by purple, and for a moment the two colours twisted together in the fire. Then the green faded and the purple remained.

"Here, Scott," said Mrs. Winch. "You try this jar and see what happens."

"Oh boy!" said Scott, as he squatted down beside her on the floor. He took the jar she offered and poured some of the powder into his hand. When he tossed it into the fire, he squealed happily. Bright red dragons danced everywhere in the flames.

Cathy and I watched totally absorbed as the two of them sat before the fire creating dragons of blue, gold, red, green and purple. The movement and colours of the fire reminded me of the northern lights. It was so beautiful that no one spoke, and the only sound was the crackling of the burning log.

Mrs. Winch replaced the jars in their box and sat quietly watching the flames return to their normal yellow-orange colour.

"Help me up, Scott," she said cheerfully, and pushed herself to a standing position using Scott's shoulder as a boost. He was so busy watching the fire that he hardly noticed her.

"What kind of chemicals are those?" I asked.

"Do you know, John," said Mrs. Winch, "I haven't any idea at all. My husband brought them one year, and I haven't used them since my own son sat with me to watch them." She was going to say more, but Scott interrupted.

"Did you see the dragons, Cathy? There were millions and trillions of them. All different colours. They were fighting together and playing in the fire. I wonder how come they didn't get burned?"

"I'm glad you liked them, Scott," said Mrs. Winch. "But I still have one more dragon to show you. You'll need to come outside, though, to see him, because he's too big to bring into the house."

I really didn't want to leave the flames, even though they weren't making dragons any more. I guess they had almost hypnotized me. But everyone else was standing up, waiting for me to come with them, so I pulled myself away.

The night air was surprisingly cool after the heat of the living room. Only the sound of crickets broke the stillness. No traffic ran on Bridge Road, and the bypass was too far away to be heard. There were no street lights this far from the town, and most of the houses were already in blackness.

"Where's the dragon?" asked Scott. He was always so impatient.

"Look up," said Mrs. Winch. Scott just stared at her. "Look up," she repeated. "In the sky. Do you see that star?" We all looked in the direction she was pointing. "It's called Eltamin, or Draconis, the Dragon's Star. That's because it's part of a group of stars called Draco, the Dragon. See the head there? And the body is all tail. It looks something like a kite — the big diamond-shaped group."

I don't think Scott really saw the shape of a dragon in the sky, and even Cathy and I had to strain our imaginations, but he was satisfied to know that somewhere up there was a dragon that had a whole bunch of names.

We stood looking at all the billion stars until I felt myself shiver in the night air. "Brr!" I said.

Cathy turned and looked toward the house. "Oh no!" she gasped. "Your house is on fire, Mrs. Winch!"

Mrs. Winch only laughed. "No it isn't, Cathy. That's just smoke from the fireplace. The chimney doesn't work very well, and I can't afford to have it repaired. The smoke sometimes comes out into the room instead of being drawn up the chimney. It looks dangerous, I know, but it really isn't. Well, I expect you children had better be heading home now. I don't want to keep you up too late."

"It's been a really neat day," sighed Scott. "I saw four dragons, counting the silk dragon at home." He stopped suddenly. "Oh no!" he said. "We forgot to bring back the stinging dragon."

"That's all right," said Mrs. Winch. "You can return it tomorrow, or the day after. There's no rush."

"We'll do that," I promised.

It was spooky walking home in the pitch blackness of the Bridge Road tunnel, with only the lights of the town ahead to guide us along under the heavy overhanging branches.

In the living room Mother was waiting for us, and we were immediately packed off to bed. I had just climbed under the covers and turned off my light when my door opened a tiny crack. I turned the lamp on again quickly. It was Scott.

"What do you want?" I asked.

"Turn off the light," he answered, opening my drapes. "I want to see the dragon in the sky. Look, John! There he is! I can't see him from my room."

I rolled over to the edge of the bed to look at the stars, and sure enough Scott had found the dragon. I hadn't even thought he understood earlier.

"Can I stay here with you?" he asked. "And watch my dragon?" Without waiting for a reply, he poked his way under my blankets and lay facing the window. Before I got time to complain, though, he had fallen asleep, so I just left him.

When I reached the woods the following morning, Steven was waiting for me. He looked impatient. "It has to be today, John," he said. "I think he plans to leave before supper time."

"Gosh," I said. "I still haven't thought of a way of getting the money out of his room. I don't even know which room he's in."

"That's something you'll have to figure out before you get there. Maybe Cathy has some ideas."

"Why don't you come with us too, Steven? You'd be able to decide things better. It would be a lot easier."

"You know I can't go across the river, John. I told you that before."

I was a little fed up with this part of the mystery. "Why not?" I demanded. "Are you afraid of getting lost?"

"No, that's not it." Steven looked hurt. "I used to live across there. I went over the river every day on my way to and from school," he said distantly. I was sorry I had asked.

"Do you ever want to go back there? To see your old house?"

"Yes," he replied, "sometimes I want to cross over. But sometimes I feel that perhaps it's better this way. If I don't go back, it will stay exactly the way it was when

I left."

"What do you mean?"

"If I go back, I'll see all the things that have changed. If I don't see them, then I'll have only memories of what they used to be like. And those memories stay the same."

"What about your friends?" I asked. "Do you miss them?"

"Yes," he said. "But they left long ago too. I haven't seen them since then."

I was vaguely aware that what Steven said probably made sense, but I wasn't sure how.

"Let's get back to our problem, John," he suggested. "You, Cathy and Scott have to sneak into the crook's room and get the money. Altogether he's taken about seven thousand dollars now and he won't have left it sitting around. You'll have to search really thoroughly."

"Seven thousand!" The thought of that much money made me dizzy. And I had to steal it back!

I ran home and found Scott and Cathy just finishing their breakfast. "Come on, you guys," I called. "It's ten thirty already and we've got a lot to do."

Scott and Cathy seemed surprised, but they agreed to come to the Inn with me. Scott wanted to drop off Mrs. Winch's stinging-dragon stick on the way there, but I told him we didn't have time. He decided to take it anyway and return it on our way home.

It was a long hike to the Inn, but I didn't want to tell

Mother we'd be late for lunch in case she started asking questions. I only hoped she wouldn't be too angry. Maybe she'd think we were safely at Mrs. Winch's and wouldn't worry about us.

There was really no choice left open now. I had made a promise to Steven.

The day was growing hotter and stickier as we reached the crest of the hill and looked down at the Inn. Scott was eager to push on, but Cathy and I sat down in the grass by the road and looked over the strange Chinese writing on the dragon stick.

Just as we were getting ready to start off again, I spotted the green station wagon pulling out of the Inn's parking lot and heading towards us.

"Hide!" I called, and we dived for the shrubs by the roadside. We lay perfectly still as the station wagon sped by in the direction of town. I was too close to the ground to see who was in the car, but I desperately hoped the crook was not leaving town. Then I knew he couldn't be — he was travelling away from the bypass, and no one except the locals would ever find their way out on the back roads.

When the car was safely out of sight we clambered out of the ditch and raced down the hill. Finally we reached the Inn and squeezed through the lilac hedge into the parking lot. The sun was really hot, and the glare from the glass and metal building dazzled us. It made it hard to look up at the balconies jutting out from each floor.

"Oh no," I said. "How do we find which room belongs to the crook? There must be a hundred of them here. We haven't got time to search all of them."

For a few moments we stood looking at each other.

"I know!" said Cathy. "Leave it to me." She pulled a key out of her pocket and held it up for me to see.

"What's that?"

"The key for my old locker at school. I carry it for good luck."

That didn't sound too bright to me. "What are you going to do with it?"

"Come on and you'll see. But keep out of sight yourself." We followed her into the cool main lobby and hid among the tropical plants near the indoor fountain. The huge leaves made perfect shields, yet we could hear everything that was going on.

Cathy sauntered over to the registration desk as if she owned the place. Using her sickeningly sweet voice, the one for selling Girl-Guide cookies, she said, "Excuse me, sir." The clerk turned around.

She handed him the key. "One of your guests dropped this on his way out. I ran after him, but he got in his car and drove away before I could stop him. It may be something important." He looked at the key.

"Do you know who it was?" he asked.

"I'm afraid I don't know his name," said Cathy, "but he drives a green station wagon. He's a small, thin man."

110

"Oh, yeah. I'll look after it. Thanks, kid." He turned to the rows of little boxes behind the desk and stuck the key in one of the slots.

Cathy turned and marched jauntily out of the lobby into the sunlight, an enormous smile on her face. As soon as the desk clerk was busy, we followed her out.

"It worked," she said. "He didn't tell me where the crook was staying, but I checked the number under the mail slot. Our crook is in room twelve. That must be on the bottom floor."

"What do we do now?"

"We sneak back in and search room twelve for the money, dummy." Cathy made it sound so easy.

"There's another door at the far end there," I said. "Let's go."

We charged across the grass and stopped outside the end doors. No one was visible through the glass, so we pushed our way through the doorway into the empty hall.

It was wonderfully cool inside. The floor was heavily carpeted and there was beautiful gold and deep-red paper on the walls. The sofas and chairs in the hall looked as if you might sink forever if you sat in one.

Scott counted off the numbers of the rooms as we passed. "Eighteen, sixteen, fourteen, here's twelve!"

"Shh!" Cathy tried the door gently. "Rats! It's locked! Now what do we do?"

"Back outside!" I whispered. "I've got an idea." I

counted off the numbers the way Scott had done.

We soon stood blinking in the bright sunlight. "What's your idea?" Cathy demanded.

I was already walking along the grass at the side of the building. "Count the balconies, Cathy. Eighteen, sixteen, fourteen — that's twelve." I pointed to a balcony partly screened by a clump of evergreen shrubs. The first-floor balconies were only a few inches off the ground, and it was no trouble to swing over the railing onto number twelve. I tried the balcony door. It was open.

"Hurry up!" I urged, poking my head into the room. The drapes were closed and the room was dim and cool. "What's taking you so long?" I added, when the others still didn't come over.

"I'm scared," said Scott. "What if that man comes?"

"He won't if we're quick. Now, get up here."

Cathy gave him a boost and they came hesitantly into the crook's room. There was another bedroom opening off the one where we stood.

"Search in here, Cathy. I'll check the other room. Scott, guard the door."

We began to rummage through everything. It was clear the crook was ready to leave. Suitcases lay open on the bed, full of clothing, and a coat in a plastic cover lay beside them. In one suitcase I found nothing but women's clothing. There were dresses and stockings, even shoes and a box with a wig in it. It must be his disguise, I thought.

Suddenly Scott and Cathy burst into the room where I was searching. "John!" Cathy whispered in panic. "There's someone at the door! What can we do?"

"Quick! Into the closet!" I pulled the door shut just as someone came in from the hallway.

'No witnesses'

The closet was stuffy with the three of us jammed in together, and Scott's hair was tickling my face. I was terrified that I would sneeze and give us away. My hand was in agony too because Cathy was partly standing on my fingers.

People were moving around in the next room. I recognized the crook's voice.

"Did you get everything you wanted at the store, Tim?"

"Naw," answered a boy's voice. "Mum always wants to look at old junk like jewellery. She won't ever take me to the toy places."

The man laughed. "Never mind, son. We'll take you in before we go home. But we have to catch the train soon, and the taxi will be waiting to take us to the station. Make sure you have all your things packed up properly. That's a good boy."

"Okay, Dad."

We heard the door to the hallway open again, and more footsteps came into the other bedroom.

"I picked up the mail," called a woman's voice. "Somebody's playing silly jokes again, dear. There's a strange key in our mail slot."

"This place really is jinxed, isn't it?" said the man. "It'll be a relief to get the train and clear right out of here. I'm glad I took the full insurance on that rented car. Those repairs might have cost us fifty dollars or so."

"Is everything packed?" asked the woman.

"Pretty well. I'll just check the drawers and make sure we haven't left anything." The man's footsteps moved into the room where we were hiding. We listened tensely as he pulled open the drawers and then slammed them shut again. Will he check the closet too? I wondered. Maybe we should have hidden under the bed.

But it was too late. The steps came closer and then a hand rattled the doorknob. There was nothing in the closet to hide us as the door swung open. I remember smiling stupidly, although I was frightened half to death. For a second or so the man remained speechless, staring at us blankly. Then he recognized me, and his face went all funny, a kind of purple colour.

"You again!" he screamed.

I grabbed Scott and bolted past him. He reached out to stop us, but Cathy clipped him from the other side, and he spun around to face her. In the sudden confusion, all three of us reached the door and barrelled

115

through it into the corridor. We had no time to stop and decide what to do, as the man and his wife were immediately after us. We veered toward the main lobby.

The woman was shrieking so loudly I thought her lungs would pop.

"Come back here!" shouted the man.

We charged down the corridor to escape.

"Stop them! Stop them!" screamed the woman.

The desk clerk and a bellboy had appeared at the end of the hallway to block our exit. "Quick!" shouted Cathy. "This way!" She darted up a stairway and we followed, coming out onto the second floor with the others still in hot pursuit, clattering up the steps. Up another flight we dashed, and then up to the fourth for good measure. Our hope was that they would waste time searching for us on the third.

Scott chose this moment to drop the dragon stick, and we had to scramble under a huge sofa to get it before he would budge another inch. When he had it safely in hand again, we heard the sounds of our pursuers coming up the last steps.

"What do we do now?" gasped Cathy.

"Try the doors," I suggested in desperation. "There must be some place to hide."

We began turning doorknobs. It was almost lunch time, and most people were out. All the doors were locked except one.

"Here," exclaimed Cathy, "this one's open."

Silently she crept into the room and Scott and I followed her just as the posse came whooping along the corridor. Scott darted right under a table without waiting to look around. I leaned against the door and breathed a long sigh of relief.

"Well, hello," said a voice. We almost went through the ceiling, we were so startled. The room wasn't vacant after all.

A tall, muscular man with fair hair and long sideburns got up from his chair and turned to face us. He was wearing a red sports shirt with matching tie, and brown flared slacks. He looked awfully rich, I thought.

"What can I do for you, children?" he asked, coming toward us. "Are you lost?" His voice was kind, and his smile made us relax.

"No," I panted. "We're not lost, we're hiding. Please don't tell on us. It's really important. We're catching a crook."

The man looked vaguely amused. "Is that so?" he asked.

"Yes," added Cathy. "The guy is a real creep, too. He cheats old ladies out of their savings. In our town alone he's swindled people out of thousands of dollars."

The man was interested. "Now, how could he do that? Does he sell them the Toronto-Dominion Centre?"

"He pretends he's a building inspector," I explained. "He tells them they need repairs, then takes their money. He says he will fix their houses, but he doesn't

117

do any work. He just disappears."

"How disgusting," said the man.

"Anyway, we know where he is. We'll use your phone to call the police, okay?"

"Well," he hesitated. "I don't know if the phone is connected right now. You see, I'm checking out today."

"Let's just try," I urged. "We can't let him escape. What should I say, Cathy?" She had moved across the room and was looking out the window. We were on the opposite side of the Inn from room twelve — Bridge Road ran along this side, and the full glare of the sun was bouncing off the glass and reflecting onto the trees.

Scott had slipped farther under the table and looked exhausted. I wondered momentarily whether he was falling asleep.

I picked up the receiver. "We've got to get that money back before he escapes. Hello? Is that the operator? . . . Oh." I turned to the man. "It's the hotel desk."

I turned back to the telephone and was just going to ask the clerk to get me the police when the man pushed down those little buttons on the telephone and cut me off. "Hey!" I squawked. "What are you doing?"

"Perhaps I can show you what you're looking for, boy," said the man, as he ruffled an envelope of bank notes under my nose.

"Huh?" I muttered. Then it slowly connected. A sickening feeling overcame me, and I could feel a faint tremor in my stomach. The money! What an idiot I had been! This guy was the real crook, and we had told him everything!

"But the car — " I stammered. "You drive a green car — "

"What do you take me for, kid?" said the man. "I have to cover my tracks once in a while, just to make the witnesses conflict. I rent different cars; I don't drive the same one more than a few days at a time. Right now I've got that orange T-bird on the lot. Anyway, for you the game's over, junior!"

Before I could move he stepped forward and grabbed me by the throat. "Call over the little girl, kid, or that'll be it." Cathy started to walk over on her own.

"Too bad you kids couldn't mind your own business. Kind of late for that now, though. I'll have to think of some way to take care of you. Don't try anything stupid; stand against the wall while I think."

He didn't seem to notice Scott crawling carefully out from under the table behind him.

"Maybe I'll just tie you up in the closet for a few months," he went on. "I'm sure your skeletons would make a nice mystery for some future guest." I had a feeling that he was playing with us, teasing us, but it didn't make me feel any less scared.

Scott was now directly behind him, with the end section removed from the dragon stick and the long silver needle aimed right at the seat of the man's brown

slacks. The crook opened his mouth to speak to us again, but we'll never know what he was going to say. With a strange look of concentration, half smile, half frown, Scott plunged the needle in.

For a moment a stunned look crossed the man's face; then, exploding into action, he howled and leaped into the air. Roaring with pain, he twisted round and grabbed Scott. But that brother of mine has had lots of practice in sneaky fighting, and the crook howled again as Scott bit him then darted to the window, keeping just out of reach.

"Scott, the door!" I yelled. But he didn't understand what I meant. Instead, he pulled open the balcony door and dashed out into the glaring sunlight. "Oh no," I groaned.

"Decoy the crook!" I called to Cathy in an undertone. "I'll get Scott." Cathy moved for the hall door, and the crook leaped after her with a roar of anger. I charged toward the balcony to get Scott.

We all failed miserably. The crook had grabbed Cathy and dragged her to the balcony door by the time I reached Scott. He pushed her roughly outside beside us, and she almost fell over the lawn chair that stood on the balcony.

"Hah!" panted the crook. "Now you're cornered, eh? You think you're so smart, you amateur detectives. Big heroes, eh? Catch the nasty bad man. Well, you won't try that again in a hurry, you brats. You're going to have a nice trip — a nice trip down four floors, and a happy landing on some hard concrete. You were afraid of the people in the hall, weren't you? You tried to climb down the balcony, didn't you? You must have slipped, mustn't you? Now, who would ever doubt that?"

He shut the door behind him and moved toward us. I hoped desperately that people driving by on the bypass or on Bridge Road would notice what was happening. Then, with a horrible feeling of despair, I remembered that with the sun's glare on the building it would be almost impossible for anyone to see us.

Frantically I looked around the little balcony for some way to escape, but there was none. The crook blocked the door to the bedroom, and there was no other exit. Between us and him were the aluminum lawn chair and a small metal table and nothing more.

"No witnesses," the crook was saying. "Everyone's at lunch. Too bad kids." There was a nasty sneer on his face as he came towards us. Scott pushed closer to me, and Cathy had turned white. Even then I felt that the crook really didn't intend to drop us over the balcony as he threatened. He was only trying to scare us, and it wasn't going to work if I could help it.

Then I got my idea. Suddenly I darted forward and seized the table. I hurled it at the crook with all my might. Unfortunately both the table and the chair were attached to the balcony rail by chains — I guess the motel owners didn't want them to get swiped. The table flew as far as the chain would let it and then bounced back toward me. In desperation I picked up the chair and balanced it on top of the table, trying to keep them between the man and me.

"Stupid kid," growled the crook. "Still going to play hero, are you?" He reached out to grab me and I felt his fingers brush my shoulder as I ducked down behind the table.

"I'll get you!" he screamed and tried to vault over the obstructions. He didn't make it. His feet landed on the chair and went through the nylon webbing to the table beneath. For a moment he balanced there, the chair wrapped about his knees. Almost without thinking, I tipped the table sideways. The crook shrieked — then toppled over the balcony railing, the chair still gathered around his legs.

Cathy screamed, and Scott looked at me with wide eyes. I just stared at them, feeling sick and horrified. I hadn't meant to push him over the balcony. It would have been better if he'd gotten away rather than fall four storeys to the ground.

All at once we heard a weak voice calling for help. I jumped to the railing and looked over. There was the crook only a few feet below. His legs were still entangled in the framework of the chair as he hung upside down. And the chair was gently swinging on the chain that secured it to the balcony railing.

"Help me, kid," the crook pleaded. "I was only joking about that other stuff. I was only trying to scare you, honest. Please help me!"

"I can't," I called down. "I'm not strong enough." The crook groaned. In his hand he clutched the envelope with the money. As he swung there bills started falling out and floating down like leaves to the ground.

"Help me," he moaned again, waving the envelope at me. "You can have all the money in this bundle." More bills fell out while I watched powerlessly, and then the whole envelope escaped from his hand, filling the air with a small flurry of money. Coloured scraps littered the lawn below.

It was not long before a shout came from down there. Someone had found a bill. The crook tried to call again for help, but began to choke and could say nothing. Beneath us the person was scrambling over the grass, shouting loudly about money on the ground. Before long the area under us was filled with people grabbing bills. They made such a noise that when the crook recovered enough to call for help again they couldn't hear him. Even Cathy and I were drowned out in the racket. I kept hoping someone would look up to see where the money had come from, but either they didn't realize it had been dropped from the balcony, or the sun blazing on the glass made it impossible for them to look up.

Once more the crook called for help, then suddenly the entire crowd fell silent. We took a moment or two to realize that a police car had pulled up at the edge of the lawn, and that two police officers were getting out. They heard the crook's shouts and looked up, shielding their eyes with their hands. The policemen pushed their way through the little crowd into the side door of the Inn.

It seemed as if they were with us on the balcony almost at once. One of them was the same officer who had wanted to do the story about me.

Carefully they reached over and hauled together on the chair. Then they grabbed the crook's legs and hauled him, chair and all, onto the balcony. He stood between them, swaying and looking terribly white. Then he caught sight of me.

"You stinking brat," he screamed. "You ruined everything! They'd never have caught me if it hadn't been for you!" He glared around at the startled police.

"What's all this about?" asked one of the officers. Realizing that they had arrived by chance and knew nothing at all about our crook, Cathy and I launched into the whole story — how he had swindled the old people; how we had made a mistake; how we would have to apologize to the other man; how scared we had been.

The man we had first thought was the crook suddenly burst into the room, followed by the desk clerk. "That's him!" he cried, pointing to me. "That's the boy I called you about! Arrest him!"

"We're really sorry about all that — " I began.

"Officer, arrest this boy!"

"But it's not John's fault," interrupted Cathy, "that the car wasn't the right one after all."

"If that kid had minded his own business, I'd be out of here by now."

"John, Cathy. I can't find the other part of the dragon stick. Where did it go?"

"Dad, are you all right? Did you catch those kids?"

The room was suddenly a babble of sound as people poured in and milled about. And since everyone was telling a different story, the policeman ordered us to wait until we reached the station so that he could sort it all out.

"You little hoodlums," hissed the wife of the man we had mistaken for the crook. "You ought to be sent to reform school." She stormed out with her husband and the little boy. I felt sorry for the trouble we had caused them and wanted to apologize, but there really wasn't anything I could do.

"Oh no!" said Cathy suddenly. "The money! The envelope fell on the ground and everyone was picking up the bills."

The policeman groaned. "I'd better get on the loudspeaker and ask everyone to hand it back in. I don't know how much we'll actually recover though."

We paraded down the corridor with our prisoner and took the elevator to the front lobby. One policeman locked the swindler in the cruiser while the other got the portable loudspeaker out of the trunk.

He blew into the mouthpiece once or twice to see if it was working. "Your attention please," he boomed. "Ladies and gentlemen, a large sum of cash has accidentally been scattered around the grounds during the last half-hour. Anyone who has any of the money is asked to return it to us immediately."

"Let me say something," I begged. The officer was a little surprised, but he held the loudspeaker for me to talk into.

"Please," I said, "the money has to come back. It belongs to old people who can't afford to lose it. They were swindled by a guy who pretended he was a building inspector. They really need the money. Please give it back."

Soon people began handing bills in to the policeman. When the flow slowed down, he thanked them and asked if anyone still had money. No one replied.

"Well," he sighed, as he finished counting the bills, "I hope it's all here. How much was there supposed to be?"

"Seven thousand dollars," I replied anxiously. Surely nobody would keep the money they found?

"I guess it's all here, then," announced the policeman. "I've counted seven thousand, one hundred and

127

twenty."

"Wow!" said Cathy.

"Yeah," I echoed, "How come?"

"It seems we've had a few donations," said the officer. "Any suggestions about what to do with the extra money?" He smiled at us.

"Let's give it to Mrs. Winch," said Cathy, "to fix her chimney. Could we?" The policeman grinned.

That's Steven!

Once the crook was safely in the station, we were driven home in the cruiser. Even when the policeman explained everything to her, Mother kept saying she just couldn't believe it.

"Come to think of it," said the officer, "I don't believe it myself. How did you kids find out about this affair? And how did you figure out where and when to go for the money?"

I explained about meeting Steven and what he told us to do — how he decided when to search the hotel, how he mixed the cars up on us, and so on.

"We'll have to get together with this Steven," said the policeman. "Where does he live?"

"I don't know."

"What's his last name, then? We can trace him pretty easily."

I had to admit that I didn't even know that much — in fact, I had no idea of how to get in touch with him.

"How about you?" The officer turned to Cathy, "Do you know anything about this boy?"

"I've never even seen the kid," she answered. "He's awfully shy, I guess. He only talks to John."

The policeman looked very disappointed. I suppose he wanted the *Village Weekly* to do a story about Steven's good deed or something.

"When you do see him again, John, get him to contact us, will you? I think you all have some kind of reward coming, even if I personally have to buy you an ice cream cone." He winked at us and smiled.

As the cruiser pulled out of our driveway, Mother hugged Cathy and me, mumbling how wonderful we were. Scott bounced about as usual, wanting his share of the attention too.

That evening the conversation was kind of weird. One minute our mother and father would be telling us how proud they were of our bravery and quick thinking, and then the next moment both of them would lecture us for being so silly as to expose ourselves to that much danger. Still, they both seemed to be pretty pleased with the results.

What with all the excitement of the day, I thought there would be no chance of getting to sleep at all that night. I remember lying in bed thinking about the day's events, and suddenly opening my eyes to find it was already morning. I must have been tired out by all that crook-catching.

"We have to go back to Mrs. Winch's today," Cathy said as I came into the kitchen. "We never did take the dragon stick back yesterday. And she'll be really interested in what happened."

Mother came into the room. "Before you go off looking for adventures again today, Mr. Hero, would you do a good deed for your mother? You know where the lawn mower is! . . ."

Groan. That would tie me up for almost an hour, so Cathy and Scott decided to go ahead without me. I agreed to meet them at Mrs. Winch's house if they promised not to tell her about the extra money until I got there. Off they went along the river trail, while I dragged the mower out of the garage. When I got through, I rushed off to join the others at Mrs. Winch's.

A short distance along the trail I met Steven.

"Hi!" I shouted. "Am I glad to see you! We're getting a reward, and the police want to talk to you."

Instead of looking happy, Steven smiled the same sad smile I had seen many times before. "I've already got my reward," he said quietly. "I came to give you this." He pointed under a half-rotten log, and all I saw at first was a mound of soft, damp moss. "It's for Scott to add to his collection."

"Come on with me to Mrs. Winch's house," I urged. "You can give it to him personally. He'd love that, and the others would be really pleased to meet you."

"You've forgotten again," he sighed, in a voice that

131

sounded hollow and far away. The look in his eyes became even more remote. "I can't cross the bridge, John. The river is wide — much wider than you could ever dream. And I must wait on this side."

"I don't understand."

"You will some day, John. But now I have to say goodbye. Maybe sometime we'll see each other again. Thank you for everything." He walked off into the trees before I could even speak.

I continued on down the trail to Mrs. Winch's, but the excitement I had felt was gone and my feet seemed somehow heavier. I had a strange feeling that I would never see Steven again and that the mystery would never really be solved. He would have made a good friend, if only he lived near here.

Mrs. Winch welcomed me very warmly when I arrived, congratulating me and thanking all of us over again for saving her house. When we explained about the extra money, she actually kissed each of us and started to cry. I was very brave about this mushy stuff, but Scott looked as if he even enjoyed it. When Mrs. Winch went into the kitchen to make some tea for me, I gave Scott his present from Steven. Carefully he looked into my hands.

"It's nothing but a lot of moss, John," he complained. "Why would — oh!" He broke off and picked up something from the moss, holding it carefully, as if it might break if he breathed. "Look, John! It's a baby dragon — a real live baby dragon!"

He held up a small brown-spotted salamander for us to see. Even Mrs. Winch, coming in with my tea, seemed impressed. "That's the best kind of dragon, Scott," she said smiling.

There was a knock at the door and Mrs. Winch went to answer it. In sailed Mrs. Ross, the lady whose grass I had cut. She held a newspaper in her hand.

"I thought perhaps you'd all be interested in this," she said. "It's the morning paper from the city."

We looked at the headline. *Dragon Children Trap Suspect,* it read. There was a photograph of Cathy and me talking to the policeman, and one of Scott picking up the missing part of the dragon stick. I didn't remember anyone taking pictures, but I probably didn't notice much in all the excitement. There was a big story, all about our adventure, and it even called us "heroes" — I didn't feel like a hero. There was a part about Mrs. Winch, saying she was "an elderly widow who owned the weapon the children used." She laughed when she read that her dragon had "bitten the suspect." The crook, who was wanted by police in four provinces, had confessed to everything.

"And another thing," continued Mrs. Ross. "You know what an old grouch Richard Kingford has been all these years. Well, this morning he came over with a bunch of his roses and gave them to me. He said that the children had opened his eyes. I think he likes me." She

133

gave a little giggle and smiled at Mrs. Winch. "I'll invite you all to the wedding."

It seemed to me that she was counting an awful lot of chicks before they hatched, but I didn't want to spoil her fun. She congratulated and thanked us all again and then sailed out of the room.

Cathy had moved to the armchair and was looking at the little framed photograph that she had picked up once before. Mrs. Winch smiled at her, the sad smile that I thought I recognized.

"Who is the boy in this picture?" asked Cathy. "He looks something like John."

"I thought so too," murmured Mrs. Winch. "That's my son. He died twenty years ago in an accident across the river, just out of town. He's been dead a long, long time, but sometimes I still take pine branches from the yard, or flowers, and put them on his grave."

I went across to Cathy and looked over her shoulder. Suddenly my knees felt shaky and my breathing became difficult. The blond hair, the freckles, the plaid shirt — everything was exactly the same. The boy in the photograph was Steven.